About the Author

Jean Ure had her first book published while she was still at school and immediately went rushing out into the world declaring she was AN AUTHOR! But it was another few years before she had her second book published and during that time she had to work at lots of different jobs to earn money. As well as writing, Jean really loves drama, acting and the theatre and in the end she went to drama school to train as an actor. Some of her ideas for the Stevie Silver stories come from her experiences there. Jean has written more than eighty books, and you can read about some of them on her website, which you can find at **www.jeanure.com**

Jean now lives in Croydon with her husband and their family of seven rescued dogs and four rescued cats.

Also by Jean Ure from Orchard Books

Stevie Silver – Stage Struck

Girls Stick Together
Girls are Groovy
Boys are OK!
Pink Knickers aren't Cool

ORCHARD BOOKS
338 Euston Road, London NW1 3BH
Orchard Books Australia
Hachette Children's Books
Level 17/207 Kent Street, Sydney, NSW 2000, Australia
ISBN 978 1 84121 782 6
First published in Great Britain in 2006
A paperback original
Text © Jean Ure 1999 and 2006
The stories in this book were first published
as part of the *Sandy Simmons* series
The right of Jean Ure to be identified as the author of
this work has been asserted by her in accordance with
the Copyright, Design and Patents Act, 1988
A CIP catalogue record for this book is available
from the British Library
3 5 7 9 10 8 6 4 2
Printed in Great Britain

Stevie Silver

STAR LIGHT

JEAN URE

ORCHARD BOOKS

Contents

Spotlight Spook

Chapter 1

Everyone was just about sick of Starlotta.

Starlotta is a girl in our class at stage school and nobody can stand her. Well, I suppose her best friend Tiffany can. But not any of the rest of us!

The reason we can't stand her is that she is always boasting and showing off and making like she's just *sooo* much better than anyone else. She has this big gross uncle that's on television. She goes on and on about him till it makes you want to scream. On and on and *on*.

She is unbearable at the best of times. But ever since she'd been given the lead in our end-of-term show she had become just about im-POSS-ible.

"I'm going to ask my uncle if he'll come to the show," she told us, all self-important, as we changed out of our practice clothes at the end of rehearsal.

(It was just us girls. The boys are so lucky! They

don't have to put up with her anywhere near as much as we do.)

"Of course," she said, "my uncle wouldn't normally come to watch drama students. But as it's me—"

"He'll come!" gushed Tiffany.

"Yes, well, I *have* got the lead," agreed Starlotta.

The show we were doing was called *Happy Families* and it was all about two sisters playing a game of snap. The sisters were Steff (who is my very, *very* best friend) and Starlotta. Starlotta reckoned she was the lead because she was the older sister and got more to do.

"I mean, if I was just a *playing* card, I wouldn't bother asking him," said Starlotta.

The rest of us were playing cards. I could see Rosa gritting her teeth and Dell rolling her eyes. (Rosa and Dell are my next best friends after Steff.)

"Well! I mean. There wouldn't really be much point, would there?" said Starlotta. "Not just for a playing card."

"No point at all," tittered Tiffany.

"That's not to say," said Starlotta, kindly, "that I won't do my best for you. I shall tell him that although you are just playing cards on *this* occasion, you have all had proper parts in your time."

"Too kind," murmured Dell.

"No, it's the least I can do," insisted Starlotta. "You don't have to thank me."

Just nearby I heard a choking sound. It was coming from Steff. Rosa was practically purple. Some of the others were looking a bit sick, as well.

"Just because we don't have *names*, doesn't mean we're not proper parts," burst out Petal.

Petal is Petal Lovejoy. She was busy tugging a comb through the tangles in her hair. (Last week her hair had been bright pink, like candy floss, this week it was a weird sort of mud colour.)

"After all," she said, pulling out some bits by the roots, "if it wasn't for us being playing cards, you wouldn't have anything to do."

Starlotta beamed. "That's *right*. You are *very important*."

"It's a bit like being the Queen," oozed Tiffany. "If it wasn't for ordinary people like us, she wouldn't have anyone to be Queen over."

Rosa planted her hands on her hips. "Who are you calling ordinary?" she said.

"I just *meant*," said Tiffany, "that being playing cards is like being ordinary people and playing the lead is like being the Queen. That's all I meant."

Rosa sniffed. "Well, if you want to think of yourself as an ordinary person..."

"But we *are*," simpered Tiffany.

"Oh, get a life!" snarled Rosa.

Rosa doesn't have any patience with Tiffany when she gets all humble and creepy. And she was more sick of Starlotta than any of us. This was because she had been hoping the end-of-term show would be a musical. Rosa loves to sing! She would almost certainly have been given the lead. But Miss Todd had said that musicals were for next year. This year we were going to dance.

That was all right by me! I enjoy dancing (so long as it's not ballet). I am not one of the best, as what I am best at is being funny. Our really best dancers are Dell and Steffi. Well, and Starlotta, I suppose. But Starlotta is nowhere near as good as Dell! Which was why Dell's playing card got to dance a *pas de deux* with Buster Wells, who is the handsomest boy in our class. Maybe in the whole school. *Very* romantic!

Starlotta might have been the lead, but she didn't get to dance with Buster.

"Big-headed twit," grumbled Rosa.

The four of us, me and Steffi, Rosa and Dell, were walking up to the tube station after rehearsal. Rosa was really mad! Hopping mad! She said, "I've had just about as much as I can take of her and her mouth clacking on all the time."

"She's a motor mouth," I said, and I made vrrrm-vrrrm noises and flared my lips.

"It's not funny," snapped Rosa. "She's getting on my nerves. And anyway, who says she's the lead? All she is, is Older Sister! She doesn't have a name any more than the rest of us."

"I guess it's because she's the one that sets things off," said Dell.

It's always Dell who tries to calm us down. Me and Rosa are quite excitable. Especially Rosa. I think it's because she has Italian blood! She glared at Dell and said, "Just setting things off doesn't make her the lead!"

"No, but you have to remember—" Steffi simpered and put on a Tiffany voice, all breathless and hushed "we are just *ordinary people*."

"And she is the Queen!"

I stopped in the middle of the pavement and dropped a curtsy. Unfortunately I hadn't noticed a woman that was walking just behind. She almost did a somersault right over the top of me! She was quite cross about it.

"For goodness' sake!" she said, and she made an impatient tutting sound. "Watch what you're doing, child!"

"Stevie, that just serves you right," said Rosa. She was in a real hump! "You know we're not supposed to show off in the street."

"Gives the school a bad name." Dell and Steffi chanted it in unison.

"I was just being an ordinary person," I said. "Just curtseying to the—"

"Oh, stop it!" said Rosa. "It's no laughing matter. That girl is seriously starting to annoy me."

She meant, of course, Starlotta. I said, "She's been seriously annoying me ever since I first met her. D'you know what she said to me? On my very first day? *And where have you come from? The dwarf casting agency?*"

Steffi and Rosa sucked in their breath. "That is so not politically correct," said Steff.

"She once had the nerve to ask *me*," said Rosa, "if I was going to specialise in playing midgets."

"Just because we happen to be small!" I swung my bag, angrily, and just missed a man that was walking past. "Instead of a great gangling ostrich like her!"

"And me," said Dell. Dell is the tallest girl in our class.

"You're not an ostrich," I told her. "You're a swan!"

It's true. Dell is not only the tallest but also the slimmest and the most beautiful. Maybe that is why she is always so cool.

Dell is a swan and Steff, I think, is a cuddly puppy. And I am a honey bear (that is what my dad says). And Rosa – well!

Just at the moment Rosa was like a little angry wasp, all buzzing and desperate to sink her fangs into someone. Not someone: *Starlotta*.

"She needs taking down a peg or two," fumed Rosa.

"If she was a balloon," I said, "we could prick her with a pin. That would burst her quick enough!"

"But she isn't," sighed Steff.

"No," I said, "she's a great big motor mouth!"

"I shall be *sick* if she carries on like this," said Rosa.

"Me, too!" I said. And we both turned and made loud being-sick noises. Yeeeurgh! Bluuurgh! Spew!

"You are *disgusting*," said Steff.

"So's Starlotta! BLUUURGH!" went Rosa.

"Maybe we should do it every time she starts off boasting?" I said.

"Yessss!" Rosa jumped up and punched the air. Let's practise...one, two, three...BLUUURGH!"

We all did it together, very solemnly, in a row.

"That's the way to deal with her," said Rosa.

Chapter 2

"She is really getting on people's nerves," I said. I was telling Mum about Starlotta. "All she ever talks about is *MY UNCLE...MY UNCLE is coming to see me.*" I did a little twirl, being Starlotta. "*MY UNCLE is going to introduce me to AGENTS.*" I did another little twirl. "*MY UNCLE — oops!*"

I broke off as a teacup went crashing off the table and on to the floor. How did that happen? It couldn't have been my fault! I wasn't anywhere near it. I hastily twirled across to the other side of the room.

"*MY UNCLE—*"

"Yes, I think we get the message," said Mum. "Thomas, hand me the dustpan and brush, there's a good boy."

"Has it broken?" I said. "Who broke it?"

"I'll give you two guesses," said Mum.

"It wasn't me," I said.

"Blame it on your friend Starlotta," said Thomas.

"She's not my friend! I can't stand her. She's so vain!"

"Maybe she's just insecure," said Mum.

Starlotta? Insecure? Ha! I did another twirl.

"Stevie, do you have to?" said Mum.

"It's what *she* does. All the time! Showing off."

"Try taking no notice," advised Mum.

"We have. It just makes her worse. It's sickening!" I put on a Starlotta voice. Loud and braying. "*I've got the leading part. You're just a pack of playing cards.*"

"I dunno why you let it get to you," said Thomas. "All you've got to do is just keep saying to yourself, *I'm Stevie Silver, and I'm going to be a S*T*A*R*.*"

I looked at him, sharply. But he was serious. Ever since I'd helped him raise money to save the cats of Cats' Cottage, Thomas really did believe that I was going to be a star. I've believed it all along. You bet! But I don't go round boasting about it. I'm not like Starlotta.

"We've decided what we're going to do," I said. "Every time she starts off, we're all going to go BLUUURGH!"

"Bluuurgh?" said Thomas.

"BLUUURGH!" I said.

"Well, that's intelligent," said Mum.

It isn't any use trying to be intelligent with people like Starlotta. You have to show them how you feel. And how we felt was *sick*.

Next day, she started off again.

"I asked my uncle," she said. "At first I didn't think he'd come. But then I told him about me dancing the lead and he said—" she flung out her arms, "in that case I will make the effort. Specially for you, Little Star!"

"*Oh!*" squeaked Tiffany.

"Bluuurgh!" went Rosa.

"He's going to bring his girlfriend with him. His girlfriend—" Starlotta paused, for effect, "–is Tracey Tindall."

"*Oh!*" squawked Tiffany.

This time I went "Bluuurgh!" as well.

Tracey Tindall is this girl with huge enormous mega-boobs that's in the soap that Starlotta's uncle is in. She plays the part of a total dimbo. I mean, like, she's really dumb. All wriggling and giggling and this great big lipsticky smile. Eyelashes that stick out like spokes. And every time she moves, her chest wobbles about. Me and Rosa despise her utterly. It's the sort of part, I think, that gives women a bad name. When I am a woman I will never play that sort of part. I'll be into kung fu!

All this time, old Motor Mouth is still wittering on.

"You'll *adore* Tracey! You'll just *adore* her. I expect she'll come backstage with my uncle and then you'll be able to meet her. She's really nice. Really, really nice."

"*Oh*," breathed Tiffany.

"Just *sooo* sweet," gurgled Starlotta. "Exactly like she is on TV."

This time, we all went "Bluuurgh!"

It didn't stop her. She just gave us this look, like we were some low form of life that had crawled out of a bin bag. Then in the *loudest* voice she announced, "I'm not going to introduce to everyone. Only to my friends."

"Bluuurgh," said Rosa. She jabbed at me.

"Bluuurgh," I said.

"Bluuurgh," said Steffi.

Dell just rolled her eyes.

"If you like," said Starlotta to Tiffany, "I could ask my uncle if we could go round the studios."

"*Oh!*" squealed Tiffany.

"I've already been round, of course. Loads of times." Starlotta gave a happy laugh. "Everybody knows me there. Lucy Danvers calls me her little mascot."

"*Oh!*" thrilled Tiffany.

"Her lucky star," beamed Starlotta.

This time I almost was sick. For real.

I suppose partly it might have been jealousy. I mean, Lucy Danvers!!! *She* is not a dimbo. She is a Household Name. And a really good actress. The thought of Starlotta knowing her was enough to turn me green. But she didn't have to boast about it!

"We'll go on a day when Lucy is there," promised Starlotta. "If we're lucky, she might let us visit her in her dressing room. I sat on her lap once when I was a baby. That's why I'm special to her."

"Oh!" simpered Tiffany.

"BLUUURGH!" went Rosa.

But it wasn't any use; it wasn't working. It was going to take more than me and Rosa saying *bluuurgh* to stop Starlotta.

"She's just getting worse and worse!" wailed Steff.

"I know! I shall go mad," I said.

Dell giggled. We all turned on her. "What's funny?"

"*I sat on her lap as a baby.*" Dell put a finger in her mouth. "Gaa gaa gaa! I bet she dribbled all over her."

"That's not funny," I said. "It's revolting!"

"Bluuurgh," said Dell.

Dell just won't ever get worked up about things. I turned in despair to Rosa.

"If she carries on like this, I shall throw up for real every time I look at her!"

"Don't you worry," said Rosa. "I'll think of something!"

Chapter 3

"Listen, listen!"

Rosa came whizzing towards us as we entered the school gate next morning.

"I've had an idea! I've had an idea!"

She was so excited she kept saying everything twice.

"Idea about what?" said Steffi.

"How to make old Motor Mouth shut up!"

We jostled round her eager to hear. We all wanted Motor Mouth to shut up! I mean, our sanity was at stake. If we couldn't find some way of gagging her, we were going to end up as total fruit and nut cases.

"I have decided," said Rosa. "I have decided! What we have to do – what we have to do – we have to haunt her. We have to haunt her!"

"Haunt her how?" said Steff.

"With a ghost! We'll make a ghost!"

I said, "A g-ghost?"

"A ghost! A ghost!"

Dell, who was standing just behind, solemnly tapped a finger to her forehead. She had obviously been told the brilliant wonderful earth-shattering idea before we arrived. She thought Rosa was already a fruit and nut case!

"Every theatre has a ghost," said Rosa. "Am I right? Am I right?"

"Mm..." I nodded, a bit doubtfully. "I s'pose."

"It's a known fact," said Rosa. "You name me one theatre that doesn't have a ghost. One theatre without a ghost!"

"I never heard of Starlight having one," said Steff.

"Of course it does! It's got to. It's old. Everything old always has ghosts. I bet if you asked your Auntie Lily," said Rosa, "she'd tell you. I bet she'd tell you!"

My Auntie Lily used to be at Starlight when she was a girl. That was centuries ago. Well, decades ago. Auntie Lily is Mum's cousin and she is quite ancient.

"But I don't remember her ever talking about any ghosts," I said.

"*Look.*" Rosa was jigging up and down in her impatience. "Just use your imagination! Use your imagination!"

"She wants us to invent a ghost and frighten Motor Mouth with it. That is her idea," said Dell.

22

It was plain that Dell didn't think much of it. But I could see that it had possibilities!

"Think of ways of making a ghost!" hissed Rosa. "We'll do it at break!"

Starlotta was in the cloakroom, motor-mouthing as hard as she could go.

"Of course I'm over the *moon* that I'm playing the lead, but it is a *huge* responsibility. I mean, I'm the one the whole thing depends on! Like when we helped raise money for the poor cats. Do you remember, Stevie?" She whirled round on me. "I had to play the lady who rescued them, because I was the only one who could do it! I was the only one you could *trust*. I suppose it's because I've had so much more experience than the rest of you."

She turned and did this great big *sickly* smile at herself in the mirror.

"I'm what my uncle calls 'an old pro'. Everyone knows that I won't fluff or dry or muff my lines."

"You haven't got any lines," said Rosa.

"Not on this occasion," agreed Starlotta. "I did last year when I was on television. I said—" she clasped her hands to her chest and contorted her face like a cow in pain, "*Please, Mummy, don't hurt me!*"

"Oh!" gasped Tiffany. "I remember that. You were brilliant!"

"Yes. Well!" Starlotta smirked, modestly. "It all comes down to experience. I expect Miss Todd

23

doesn't feel the rest of you have done enough work yet to be trusted with lines."

I looked at Rosa. Rosa looked at me. We nodded. The time had come!

At first break we all met up in a corner of the playground.

"I know what we can do," said Rosa. "I know exactly what we can do!"

"Try to tell us without keeping on repeating yourself," urged Steff.

"Yes, yes! All right, all right! Now, listen. Just listen!"

We listened. This was Rosa's plan.

1. We would invent a ghost by recording some ghostly moans and wails on Dell's mum's old Walkman that she'd recently told Dell she could have.

2. On Saturday, which was the night of the performance, we would hide the Walkman in the props room, which is right next door to the Green Room. (The Green Room is like our sitting room where we all go and relax when we are not on stage.)

3. As soon as Starlotta was all by herself in there, we would switch on the ghastly wails and...

"Frighten the life out of her!" Rosa beamed at us, triumphantly. "What do you reckon?"

Tap went Dell's finger against her forehead.

"It sounds a bit complicated," muttered Steff.

"It isn't complicated! I've got it all worked out. It's

all worked out! The show starts off with you and Motor Mouth. Right?" Steffi nodded. "Then you leave the stage and all the playing cards come on."

"Right."

"So! If you just hung about in the wings with the rest of them, that'd mean Motor Mouth was all by herself in the Green Room. 'Cos she always goes to the Green Room. She lies there on the floor and does her stupid exercises."

"She thinks it's professional," I said.

"She's just showing off," said Steff.

"She's *always* showing off," said Rosa.

"OK! So when do we turn on the Walkman?" I said.

"*Then!* While she's in the Green Room."

"But we'll be on stage," I said.

"We won't, we won't!" Rosa was leaping about, almost purple in the face. "You and me are the last to go on!"

"Oh. Yes! So we are," I said.

Suddenly, Rosa's zany plan was beginning to make a bit more sense. I could see what she had in mind.

After Steffi and Starlotta left the stage the playing cards came on in pairs, one after another, to do their own little dances. Me and Rosa (being the smallest) were the Terrible Two, all dressed up as repulsive little kids with bows in our hair. We didn't mind being repulsive little kids. We loved our dance because it was funny! But because of being the smallest, we were the very last pair to come on. That meant we could easily slip into the props room and switch on the Walkman.

"It won't give you much time," said Steffi.

"It will, it will!" Rosa danced a little jig of triumph. "Everyone's dance lasts fifty seconds. I know, 'cos Miss Merchant timed us. There are six pairs, not counting me and Stevie, so that means we'll have—"

"At *least* five minutes," I said.

"At least five minutes," said Rosa. "If we can't frighten the life out of her in five minutes – well! We oughtn't to be here, that's all I can say!"

At Starlight, she meant. We were training to be actors!

"You don't think it's a bit mean?" said Dell. "Frightening her just before she has to make her entrance?"

"No," said Rosa. "She deserves to be frightened."

"Anyway, it's her own fault for sneaking off to the Green Room," I said. "She only does it to be grand. Nobody else does."

"She just likes to be *different*."

"Maybe it'll teach her a lesson," I said. "She'll be shaking so much she won't be able to dance properly."

I did a few wobbly steps across the playground. Rosa shrieked.

"Then let her uncle call her an old pro!"

"When shall we start the ghastly wails?" I said.

We decided we would do it the next day, in the lunch break. Dell said that we could borrow her Walkman, but she didn't want to help with the recording as she didn't think it was fair to frighten someone just before they had to go on stage. Not even Starlotta.

Steff was in two minds. She said that she was "fighting her conscience". But that afternoon, during rehearsal, Starlotta was even more horrid than usual. She actually yelled at Steff for getting her steps wrong! She apologised afterwards, but the apology was even worse than the yelling.

All sugary sweet, she said, "I'm really sorry I lost my temper with you. It's just *so* difficult for me, having to work with people who haven't had much experience. I expect too much of them! But I must learn to be more patient. It's not fair to shout at you."

After that Steffi said she didn't care if Starlotta was scared silly. The more scared, the better.

"Take her down a peg or two!"

Rosa said that we must all spend the evening practising moans.

"And wails," I said.

"They've got to be *really ghostly*," said Steff.

I practised my ghostly wails in my bedroom. Both of our cats were with me. Sheba was sitting in a heap on top of the wardrobe, Bunter was curled up on my duvet. Neither of them took the slightest bit of notice! I wailed and I howled and they didn't even twitch an ear. Then Thomas came and thumped on my door and said, "When you've finished playing at ghosts, Mum said to tell you tea's ready."

"If you'd heard me at dead of night," I said, "would you have though I was a real ghost?"

"No," said Thomas.

"Why not?" I said.

"'Cos I don't believe in ghosts," said Thomas.

Honestly! My brother! He has *no* imagination. As for the cats – well! Everyone knows you can't fool a cat. They're far smarter than Starlotta!

Next day, in the lunch break, me and Steff and Rosa shut ourselves away in one of the music rooms. Rosa had asked Miss Todd if we could. She'd told her we had some recording to do. Which of course was true!

"I just hope she doesn't want to listen to it," giggled Steff.

We all had a go at moaning and wailing. Rosa was by far the best.

" o o O O O O o , " she went, into Dell's Walkman.

When me and Steffi did it, it sounded like people just pretending to be ghosts. When Rosa did it, it sounded like the real thing! Really creepy.

Really sssssspine ch-ch-chilling!

I wanted to add some clanking chains, but Steffi said that would ruin it. She said, "It's perfect, just as it is."

"D'you reckon it'll scare her?" said Rosa.

"It scares me!" said Steff. "Play it again! I love that bit where your voice goes all high and quavery, like the blood's draining out of you...yes! That bit!"

" o O O O O O o , " wailed Rosa's voice, out of the Walkman. Steffi and me clutched at each other.

"That'll scare her *stupid*," said Steffi.

Chapter 4

It was Saturday night and we were all in the dressing room, changing into our costumes ready for the performance. The curtain was due up in half an hour. As usual, everyone was quite tense!

"I think I'm going to be sick," announced Petal. "My tummy's full of butterflies."

We were all full of butterflies. Rosa said that she could feel them, flittering and flutting. She meant fluttering and flitting! Steffi said that hers were more like moths than butterflies. *Giant* moths. "Batting at me with their wings!"

Tiffany was in a panic because she couldn't remember any of her steps. Someone else was in a panic because she'd left her lucky mascot at home. Even Starlotta, for once, had stopped motor-mouthing.

"Blank!" moaned Tiffany. "I'm a total blank!"

"It's only stage fright," I said.

"Only?" screeched Tiffany.

"As soon as you get out there, your feet will get their memory back."

"They won't, they won't! It's gone completely! What am I going to do?"

Tiffany turned piteously to Starlotta, her *best friend*. But old Motor Mouth was too busy prinking and preening in front of the mirror to care about Tiffany.

"Don't let it get to you," advised Rosa. "You don't want to end up like the Ghost Girl, do you?"

Tiffany gaped at Rosa through the mirror.

"What G-Ghost Girl?"

"One that haunts the Green Room," said Rosa. "Tell them about her, Stevie! You were the one who discovered her."

By now the whole dressing room was gaping at us – including Dell and Steffi. Me and Rosa had made up our story of the Ghost Girl during the rehearsal yesterday. Even Steffi didn't know about it!

"Go on," said Rosa. "Tell 'em!"

"Well, it was this girl," I said, "way back in history—"

"When in history?" That was Starlotta suddenly coming to life.

"Oh," I said, "about—"

"Sixty years ago," said Rosa.

"Yes! When the school first started."

"So what happened to her?"

"She got this terrible stage fright," I said. "She was just so scared she couldn't go on. She just sat in the dressing room and wept. And she didn't have any understudy so one of the others had to take over and read her part for her."

"She was so ashamed," said Rosa, "she went and hanged herself in the Green Room."

A gasp went up. Tiffany gave a little screech. Rosa continued, ghoulishly. "By the time they found her, it was too late. She was dead."

Tiffany's eyes swam like two huge satellite dishes in the middle of her white clown's make-up.

"Now she haunts the Green Room," I said. "The first night of every performance, she's there."

"Doing what?" said Starlotta.

"What ghosts do...wailing and moaning and wringing her hands."

Starlotta tossed her head. "I haven't heard of her!"

"That's probably because no one's seen her for a while," I said.

"So how do you know she's still around?" whispered Petal.

"Because people have *heard* her."

A hush fell over the dressing room.

"You're just making it up," said Starlotta.

"Well, if that's what you want to think," I said.

"All right!" Starlotta swivelled round on her chair.

"Who told you?"

I very nearly gave the game away by giggling. It was Rosa who said, "Her Auntie Lily told her."

Three cheers for Auntie Lily! Now even Starlotta would have to believe it.

"Did Auntie Lily actually see her?" said Dell. She said it very solemnly.

I stifled my giggles. "Oh, yes," I said. "The Ghost Girl was quite a common sight in those days. I expect she's faded a bit by now. That's why you only get to hear her voice, moaning and carrying on."

"Oh, help!" cried Petal. "I never knew we had a ghost!"

"Wouldn't be a proper theatre without a ghost," said Rose.

"But I'm scared of them!" wailed Petal.

"I'm not," said Starlotta. "Ghosts can't hurt you. Anyway, it's all rubbish!"

Promptly at half-past seven, the curtain went up. Me and Rosa stood in the wings, watching as Younger Sister and Bossyboots (Steffi and Starlotta) did their opening number.

"You don't think we've frightened her off?" hissed Rosa. "Telling her about the ghost?"

"No!" I said. Starlotta was made of sterner stuff than Tiff or Petal. She wouldn't be so easily scared. Not until she actually heard for herself...

I was right! The two Sisters came running off and

Steffi took up her position in the wings. Starlotta, as usual, headed for the Green Room. It is right next to the stage and she just loves to shut herself away in there and make like she's too important to mingle with the rest of us. What she'd *really* like is a dressing room all of her own with a great big star on it.

"Quick!" Rosa grabbed my arm. This was our cue! We tore down the passage to the props room.

The props room is really just a little cubby hole. It has one door that opens off the passage and another that opens on to the Green Room.

We'd hidden the Walkman in there earlier, under a load of old masks, and opened the door to the Green Room just the tiniest crack, to let the ghostly sounds go wailing through.

We didn't dare turn the light on, which meant we had to do everything just by feel. It is *really crowded* in the props room. Props all over the place! But we managed to crawl across the floor on our hands and knees and dig the Walkman out from under the masks. Then Rosa pressed the playback button and we crouched together in the darkness, awaiting results.

"o O O O O O o," howled Rosa's voice, into the Green Room.

"Who's that?" said Starlotta, sharply.

Rosa and me jabbed at each other with our elbows. It was working!

"O O o h ," wailed the ghost.

"Who is it?" shrieked Sarlotta. "Who's there?"

"O O o h !"

I had to stuff my fist into my mouth to stop myself from squealing. We'd meant to rush off and leave the tape playing, but we couldn't tear ourselves away! Seconds later we heard the door of the Green Room slam, and Starlotta's feet go clattering past in a panic. Hooray! We'd done it! We'd silenced the Motor Mouth!

Rosa prodded at me. "Let's go!"

We raced back just in time as the Clowns came off. They were the last couple before us. Phew! We'd almost missed our entrance.

Starlotta was standing in the wings. I thought she looked a bit white and shaken but I didn't really have time to do more than just glance at her. Me and Rosa did our Terrible Two number – clap hands, stamp feet, turn around, clap again – we got a burst of applause! – and then the two Sisters came running back on.

I could see right away that Starlotta had been frightened. She was off balance and her timing was all wrong. It was exactly what we'd wanted! We'd set out to teach her a lesson. Take her down a peg. Now we'd done it and I should have been feeling really pleased. But I wasn't.

Starlotta's uncle was out there, and old dimbo

Tracey. Poor old Motor Mouth! She'd been so desperate to make a good impression, and we'd gone and ruined it all for her.

I knew Rosa would say she deserved it. She did deserve it! All the same, I couldn't help thinking that maybe Dell was right and it was a mean trick to have played.

But then, quite suddenly – zap! Starlotta was back! It was like she'd never heard the ghostly wails. Like she'd never gone tearing off in a panic out of the Green Room. She'd pulled herself together. She was a real old pro!

I admired her for that. It didn't make me *like* her; but I had to admit, she'd got what it takes. It's what Auntie Lily says about people. People she approves of. "They've got what it takes!"

Me and Rosa exchanged glances. Rosa pulled a face. A Terrible Two sort of face. It seemed that Starlotta really was unsquashable.

At the end of the show, when the game had been played and Bossyboots had won, all the playing cards went whirling off into the wings. Steffi and Starlotta did their final number, then pair by pair the playing cards danced back. First the Young Lovers, then the Morris Dancers, then the Jugglers, then the Clever Clogs, then the Jumping Beans, then the Clowns, then me and Rosa, the Terrible Two. Last again!

We had about two minutes before we had to make our entrance.

"Let's go get the Walkman!" hissed Rosa.

We hurried off down the passage. We reckoned we'd just about got time to snatch the Walkman and rush it back to the dressing room before the Clowns had finished their dance.

We reached the props room and we snatched up the Walkman. We came back out in the passage... and we froze. A foot was sticking out of the Green Room wall!

Rosa clutched at me. I clutched at Rosa.

"W-w-w-w-w—"

I tried to speak, but I couldn't. My lips were trembling. My legs were trembling. All of me was trembling!

Rosa was shaking so much her teeth were chattering.

Slowly, as we stood clutching each other, the foot stepped out of the wall and into the passage. It was followed by a leg, and then an arm, and finally a body. It was a girl! Very faint and shimmering, all dressed up like Alice in Wonderland.

A girl had walked through the Green Room wall!

"Eeek!" screeched me and Rosa, at the tops of our voices.

And then we turned and ran.

Chapter 5

We arrived back, panting, in the wings.

"What was it?" gasped Rosa.

"I d-d-d-d—"

"Was it a ghost?"

"I d-d-d-d— "

"A *real* ghost?"

"I d-d-d-d— "

My lips were still trembling. My legs were still trembling. And we still had the Walkman!

I snatched it off Rosa just in time. Another second she'd have gone running on stage with it clutched in her hand. But now that I had it I couldn't think where to put it, so I did the stupidest thing…I pulled up my skirt and stuffed it down the front of my tights! It is *really* uncomfortable, dancing around with a Walkman stuffed in your tights.

All the same, I don't think it was because of the

Walkman that I fell over; I think it was because of my legs being so trembly. Me and Rosa raced on to that stage like we were running in the Olympic Games. First Rosa skidded, then I did. Rosa was just pulling herself up when I went crashing into her. Which was when I fell over…

I landed on my bottom with my legs in the air. The audience roared! They thought it was part of the act. They thought it was the Terrible Two, being funny.

Well! I scrambled to my feet and tried to clap hands, the way we were meant to, but by now Rosa had gone spinning away in the opposite direction. By the time she'd come round in a circle, I was off doing another bit. We just couldn't get ourselves together! While I was stamping, Rosa was clapping: while I was spinning, Rosa was stamping. It was a total *CAT-astrophe*.

The audience were just falling about. I could hear people giggling. There was a man in the front row who had this great honking laugh like a goose.

"Honk-onk-onk!" he went as me and Rosa skittered about the stage. We were, like, demented. Instead of clap, stamp, turn, clap, we were going clapstamp-turnclap-stamp, all out of control. Rosa stuck her finger in my eye and I trod on her foot and the Walkman kept digging into me. It was horrible!

Even people on stage were starting to titter. That was the *worst* thing. They knew we weren't being funny on purpose!

As we came off stage, both Miss Todd and Miss Merchant were waiting for us.

"What happened?" cried Miss Merchant.

Everyone stood around, eager to hear.

"Um—"

"Ah—"

Rosa rubbed a finger to and fro across her forehead. I twizzled a piece of hair round to my mouth and tried to chew. It's this thing that I do when I can't think what to say. I caught it from Steff, who does it all the time.

"We're waiting," said Miss Todd. She said it quite nicely, but you could tell she wasn't exactly pleased.

"Well, um…"

"Ah…"

"I feel sure," said Miss Todd, "that you wouldn't deliberately turn the whole thing into a farce."

I gulped and twizzled. Rosa stood on one leg, like a stork.

"Well?" said Miss Todd.

We could have told her about the arms and legs coming out of the Green Room wall. About the strange, shimmering girl dressed up as Alice in Wonderland. And us bolting back to the wings in a panic. But I think we both had this feeling that Starlotta would jeer. She'd just be so superior! After all, she'd heard ghostly wailings and it hadn't ruined her performance. Me and Rosa had just gone to pieces. And we were the ones that had started it all!

"Rosa, stand properly on two legs," said Miss Todd. "And Stevie, stop tugging at your hair! That's better. Now! May *we please* have an explanation?"

Rosa drew a deep quivering breath. I swallowed. We both started to gabble at the same time.

"We didn't—"

"We couldn't—"

We stopped.

"I'm waiting," said Miss Todd.

"We nearly missed our entrance!" blurted Rosa. She said afterwards that it was the only thing she could think of. I couldn't very well get mad at her 'cos I couldn't think of anything at all. But at Starlight, missing your entrance is a Number One Crime.

Miss Todd's lips went all pursed and puckered as if she'd sucked on a lemon. We knew what that meant. It mean TROUBLE.

"We shall talk about this later," she said.

"We could always tell her you were feeling sick," suggested Rosa, as we trailed our way back to the dressing room.

"Why me?" I squealed.

"You were the one that fell over."

"Only 'cos you went and turned the wrong way!"

"You didn't have to bash *into* me," said Rosa.

"I couldn't help it! All your arms and legs were flying about."

"Well, but you're not blind, are you?"

"Children, children!" Starlotta went prancing past us. "I hope you're not going to fall out?"

We watched, glumly, as Starlotta danced her way along the passage.

"Maybe we should just tell the truth," said Rosa.

"You mean—"

"About what we saw."

"She'll never believe us!" I bleated.

"But it's the truth," said Rosa. "People have to believe you when you tell them the truth!"

Inside the dressing room, everyone was shrieking. We always shriek when we've just done a performance. But as soon as me and Rosa walked in, the whole room went silent. And then Starlotta spoke.

"I don't want to embarrass you," she said, "but honestly, Stevie, you've gone the most peculiar shape."

Everyone turned to look at me. I looked at me, too; in the mirror. The Walkman had slipped right down one of the legs of my tights! It was sticking out in a great shelf above my right knee.

I have never felt so stupid in all my life. I had to take off my tights, *with* the Walkman in them, with everybody watching me. They didn't get to see the Walkman 'cos I bundled it up out of sight. But I had to pretend that I'd popped a muscle and it had suddenly gone back into place.

"*Weird*," said Tiffany.

As soon as I'd changed I went racing off to the stage door to meet Mum and Dad and Thomas. I tell you, I just wanted to get out!

Auntie Lily was with Mum and Dad. She's ever so loyal, she always comes to my performances. And she always insists that we go out to supper afterwards! She says that is what theatre people do.

Usually I love to go out to supper with Auntie Lily, but tonight I was just feeling so ashamed of myself. All I wanted to do was crawl into a deep dark hole and hide.

Thomas was really nice about the performance, nicer than I'd ever known him.

"You were brilliant," he said. "You were the best thing in it! You and Rosa. That bit where you bumped into each other and you fell splat, on your bum!" He chortled happily at the memory. "That was great!"

Thomas thought it was all part of the act. So did Mum and Dad. Auntie Lily was the only one who wasn't fooled.

"Stevie, let us go and wash our hands," she said. And she took me by the arm and marched me across the restaurant. No one thought it odd because everyone knows Auntie Lily is a bit eccentric.

"Now," she said, "tell me what went wrong!"

So I did. It all came pouring out of me, about the arms and the legs and the Alice in Wonderland girl and how terrified we'd been.

"Oh, my dear!" Auntie Lily dabbled her hands under the hot air machine. "You shouldn't have been terrified. The poor little soul is quite harmless!"

"P-poor little soul?" I said.

"Little Alice! She's a very friendly ghost."

My mouth fell open. "You mean, she's – *real*?"

"As real as a ghost can be! She haunts the Green Room, especially on first nights. I'm surprised you haven't met her before!"

I gulped. "She didn't hang herself because of stage fright, did she?"

"Bless you, no! She got knocked down by a taxi cab. Such a tragedy! She'd just played the part of Alice and everyone said she was going to be a big star. Next time you see her," said Auntie Lily, cosily, "be sure to give her my love."

I reported all this to Rosa on Monday morning, as we waited outside the office to have our talk with Miss Todd.

"Auntie Lily says if we see her again we're to give her her love."

But Rosa only shuddered and said, "I don't ever want to see a ghost again as long as I live!"

I knew how she felt.

Show Stealer

Rosa's Cockney Rhyming Slang

Apples and pears	*stairs*
Cogs	*curlers*
Barnet (short for Barnet Fair)	*hair*
Rosie (short for Rosie Lee)	*tea*
German (short for German band)	*hand*

Chapter 1

Something was wrong with Rosa. We were all getting really worried about her.

Rosa is one of my friends at Starlight, the stage school that I go to. She is usually very bright and sparky and makes us laugh, but just lately she had started to snap and lose her temper at the least little thing. I mean, she has always been quite an impatient sort of person. Like, there is this loud-mouthed girl called Starlotta in our class. She gets on everybody's nerves. We all mutter about her, but Rosa does more than just mutter. She *explodes*! But at the same time she has this really great sense of humour, which is why we all like her.

It was her sense of humour that had suddenly gone missing, and that was why we knew there had to be something wrong. Rosa without a sense of humour is like – like lemonade without any fizz! Like a ball without a bounce.

One morning me and Steffi turned up at school to find Rosa with bright green stripes in her hair.

"Cripes!" I said. "Stripes!"

I thought that was quite funny, actually. But Rosa just glared.

"What have you done to yourself?" cried Steff.

"What's it look like I've done?" growled Rosa.

"Dyed your hair in green stripes!"

"Like a sort of sicky-delic zebra," I said. I always used to think the word was sicky-delic. I know now that it's spelt p-s-y-c-h-e-d-e-l-i-c and it's pronounced *syker-delic*. But I still think sicky-delic is better! Specially when it's bright green.

Once upon a time Rosa would have started doing zebra noises and trotting round the playground, making people laugh. Today she snapped, "You can talk, Stevie Silver! You're hardly a picture. You look like a pudding." And then she added the final insult: "A *currant* pudding!"

She was referring to my freckles. And the fact that my face is rather roundish. I like to think of it as cheeky. It doesn't look in the least like a pudding!

"Oh!" said Steffi. "Nasty!"

Rosa just made a trumpeting noise and went stalking off across the playground. We looked at Dell, who is Rosa's best friend.

"What's her problem?" said Steff.

"I think she's feeling a bit sensitive," said Dell.

"Well, you would," I said, "with green stripes in your hair!" You wouldn't just feel sensitive, you'd feel *ridiculous*, I would have thought. "What'd she do it for?"

"I dunno. Just felt like it, I s'pose."

"*How* did she do it?" said Steff. She sounded almost eager. As if she might want to put stripes in her own hair.

"She put this bath cap thing on her head and cut all holes in it," said Dell. "Then she pulled bits of hair through the holes and dyed them with green dye."

"Man, that is so weird!" I said.

"But sort of fun, in a way," said Steff. "Maybe we could all do it! I could have pink stripes and Dell could have blue and Stevie could be...orange!"

I didn't want to be orange. I said, "My mum would kill me, and anyway she'd only get mad at us for copying her. Rosa, I mean. She gets mad at everything these days." I had a sudden idea. "Maybe she is mad! Maybe that's why she's gone all green and stripey."

"Or maybe she's just trying to change her image," said Dell.

"What for?" I said. "What's she want to change her image for?"

Rosa has a perfectly good image! She is a bit on

49

the short side – like me, alas – and very tiny and spidery, and it's true she isn't beautiful like Dell, or pretty like Steffi, but she has this lovely thick black hair (at least, she did before she put the stripes in it) and huge big dark eyes that she gets from her dad, who is Italian.

"I liked her the way she was!" I wailed.

Everyone kept making comments about Rosa's hair. Even the teachers. Mr Watts, who is our class teacher and can be quite witty, said, "Dear me, Rosa! And what are you today? Girl with Green Snakes in her Hair?"

Mrs Trevor, in the office, wanted to know if she was about to star in some kind of shampoo commercial.

As a matter of fact we'd been sent for an audition just last week; but it was for a television show, not a commercial. So *that* wasn't why she'd done it.

Rosa couldn't very well snap at the teachers, but she didn't half snap at everyone else. Even poor old Petal Lovejoy, who is really quite a harmless sort of person. All Petal said was, "I like your hair!"

Petal probably *did* like her hair. She dyes hers a different colour almost every week. But Rosa obviously thought she was being sarcastic 'cos she snarled, "Pity I can't say the same for yours!"

It was ever so unkind. Petal had just had this terrible disaster. She'd tried dyeing her hair silver and it had come out as a truly horrible slush colour. She was feeling really self-conscious, so it was mean of Rosa to say what she did. But that was the way Rosa was these days.

That afternoon she had a right go at Starlotta. We were changing after dance class and Starlotta suddenly looked across at Rosa and said, "Seen any good ghosts lately?"

I knew there was going to be trouble. I mean, Starlotta was deliberately goading. See, what happened was a little while ago me and Rosa had tried to frighten Starlotta by inventing a ghost. We'd done it because we were so sick of her and her big mouth, always carrying on. Unfortunately it hadn't worked. *We'd* seen a ghost, instead! A real one. And it had scared us silly!

Somehow word had got out – you can't keep any secrets at stage school. So now, if ever Starlotta wants to get at us, she asks if we've seen anything.

"I thought you didn't believe in ghosts?" said Rosa.

"Oh, *I* don't," agreed Starlotta, all smooth and silky. "But I know *you* do! You and Stevie." She smiled at us, sickly sweet. "I thought maybe you'd seen another one, and that's what's made your hair go that peculiar colour."

Rosa just hurled herself at her. It took Dell and Steffi to haul her off. And you'll never guess what... she'd actually yanked out a long blond strand of Starlotta's hair!

Ordinarily I'd have been quite glad that someone had managed to give Starlotta what my gran would call her "come-uppance". She deserved it! But I was just so worried that she would go to Miss Todd, because then Rosa would be in real trouble. We're not supposed to go round bashing one another; not even the boys. Miss Todd always says that we represent, "Both the school and the entire theatrical profession". That means we are supposed to act like ladies and gentlemen. Not rogues and vagabonds.

"If you want respect, you must earn it."

That is what Miss Todd says. She gets really mad if she catches people brawling or name-calling.

I told Mum about it when I got home. Mum said it sounded to her as if Rosa had true fighting spirit.

"You mean," I said, "that it's *all right* for her to beat Starlotta up?"

"Well – no!" admitted Mum. "She shouldn't have gone that far, though from what you tell me it wasn't an actual fight. And I must say, Starlotta does sound a very annoying sort of person."

"She is," I said. "But Rosa's doing it to everyone!"

"What, beating them up?" said Mum.

"No, but being ratty."

"It's the theatrical temperament," said Thomas.

Thomas is my brother. He knows *nothing* about the theatre or theatrical people. He isn't interested. He's going to be a vet.

"You're always reading in the paper about big stars getting drunk and smashing the place up. You wait till you're one," said Thomas.

"I won't behave like that!" I said.

"Then you won't get to be a big star," said Thomas.

I wondered if it was true, and the only way you could become a star was to have the theatrical temperament and go round pulling people's hair out. I decided that it wasn't. 'Cos if it was, that would mean Rosa was going to be one and not me! And I most certainly *am*. I am going to have my name in lights.

✳ ✳ ✳ ✳ ✳ ✳ ✳ ✳ ✳ ✳
STEVIE SILVER
✳ ✳ ✳ ✳ ✳ ✳ ✳ ✳ ✳ ✳

So there! Thomas didn't know what he was talking about. And I was *still* worried about Rosa.

Chapter 2

Starlotta didn't go to Miss Todd, so that was a relief. She may be a boasting big mouth and get on everyone's nerves, but she is not a tittle tattle. She must have known it was partly her fault for having a go at Rosa. I suppose it means that there is some good in everyone. Even Starlotta!

Rosa never apologised for pulling her hair out. She just tossed her head and said, "I'll do it again if she gives me any hassle!"

"You'll be for it if Miss Todd catches you," I said.

"Think I care?" said Rosa.

"You ought to!" I said.

She is always telling *me* to watch it, like when I start dancing in the street or doing some of my funny impersonations. (I can do Miss Todd, dead easy. And Starlotta, no problem!) But dancing in the street isn't anywhere near as bad as pulling someone's hair out.

If Rosa wasn't careful she'd get herself in the Order Mark book again. She'd already been in there once this term, for swinging off the hot water pipes in the girls' cloakroom.

"She's going completely batty," said Steff.

"Completely doolally," I said.

Doolally is a word that my dad uses. I'm not absolutely certain what it means, but I like the sound of it. Rosa was *definitely* doolally!

Dell said that when the afternoon break came she would try talking to her and see if she could find out what was wrong. But then, all of a sudden, whiz bang! Rosa seemed like she was back to being her old self. Cracking jokes, zizzing around, making people laugh.

"What does the Queen do when she burps? *Burp*," went Rosa, being the Queen. "She issues a royal pardon!"

"Listen, listen! What's yellow and dumb? Thick custard!"

"Knock, knock! Who's there? Donna. Donna who? Donna aska stoopid questions!"

"Pathetic," yawned Starlotta.

OK, so they were quite silly sort of jokes, but some people can tell silly jokes and still make you giggle. It was so lovely to have Rosa back again! I just hoped she would stay back. But she didn't. Last class of the afternoon was Voice with Miss Marshall. Voice is where you do voice exercises – *mi mi mi mi mi, ma ma ma ma ma* – and learn to speak c.l.e.a.r.l.y and to **p r o j e c t** right to the back row of the stalls.

After we'd done the usual warm-ups Miss Marshall said we were going to try being "different sorts of people" saying things in different sorts of voices.

"Stevie!"

I jumped up immediately. I like to be chosen first! Some people don't; they like to wait and see what everyone else is going to do. It makes them nervous if they're the first one. Not me! I'm never nervous.

Miss Marshall wanted me to say '*Mary Mary quite contrary*' in my normal voice and then say it like an old person. So I did. First time round I said it quite fast. Second time I did it a bit more s...l...o...w...l...y, with a bit of a croak, *Mary Mary quite contrary*, making my voice go all wispy and faint. Everyone laughed, including Miss Marshall.

"Good! Have you any idea, Stevie, why I asked you to do that?"

I made my eyes go very big and said, "No!"

"It was to stop you gabbling! You're like an express train...you roar through life at a hundred miles an hour! Right, Starlotta. Let's have you!"

She wanted Starlotta to recite, '*Baa Baa Black Sheep*', first as her normal self and then as someone begging for mercy.

I suppose she did it quite well. On the whole. But it was really funny when Miss Marshall asked her if she had any idea why she'd been told to do it like someone begging for mercy.

"I can't *imagine*," said Starlotta.

"How about the others?" Miss Marshall looked at the rest of us, and we all giggled. We knew why!

"Took *her* down a peg or two," whispered Steffi, in my ear.

Miss Marshall advised Starlotta to "Go away and think about it."

Buster Wells (he is our heart throb) had to recite 'Little Tommy Tucker' as if he was "all covered in spots with a wart at the end of your nose."

That was funny, too! Buster isn't exactly vain, but there are times, if you ask me, when he fancies himself a little too much.

Ricky Robson, who has a head like a turnip and turns everything into a joke, had to do 'Simple Simon' as if he was a vicar, in church. He was supposed to do it seriously, but he couldn't! Miss Marshall said, "Go away, Ricky, and think of something very sad. Then come back and do it again." So he did, and it still wasn't serious. Miss Marshall asked him what he'd been thinking about, and he said, "The day my dad bashed his thumb with a hammer."

"Was that sad?" said Miss Marshall.

Ricky said yes, 'cos it broke the hammer and his

dad couldn't afford a new one. After that, Miss Marshall gave up!

Steffi had to do 'Little Polly Flinders'.

"I want you to try and sound mean," said Miss Marshall.

Steff is never mean! She is a very warm, cuddly sort of person. She did her best, but when Miss Marshall asked us what we thought, we all agreed with Dell: "She was like a grumpy teddy bear!"

"Yes," said Miss Marshall. "Not very convincing! Next time we shall have to do something to make her angry. All right, Dell, your turn! '*Jack and Jill*', please – and I want you to make it really exciting!"

We laughed at that because Dell is always so cool. She never screams and shouts like the rest of us. But Dell is a really good actress and Miss Marshall said that it was a brave attempt.

And then we came to Rosa. Miss Marshall wanted Rosa to do '*Humpty Dumpty*', like a princess.

Well! I don't think Rosa even tried. She just *gabbled.* Miss Marshall stopped her before she was even half way through.

"Rosa," she said, "have you ever heard a princess speaking like that?" I think she meant, in a Cockney accent.

"Don't see why they shouldn't," said Rosa.

"Does it seem very likely, would you imagine?"

"Don't see why not," said Rosa.

She argued and argued. She would never have dared do it with Miss Todd! But Miss Marshall puts up with A LOT.

"All right, Rosa," she said. "Try something else. Try saying this," she wrote something on a bit of paper, "in your normal voice."

Rosa looked at what Miss Marshall had written. "I wenn up the apples an' pears wiv cogs in me barnet an' a cuppa Rosie in me German." We all applauded!

"Good," said Miss Marshall. "Now as a princess."

Rosa opened her mouth. "Ay went up the *stay*-ahs with *curl*-ahs in may *hay*-ah AN' A CUPPA TEA IN ME 'AND!"

"Did that sound like a princess?" said Miss Marshall.

Solemnly, we shook our heads. Rosa turned scarlet. "I don't wanna sound like some stupid princess!"

"Just as well," muttered Starlotta. "Certainly don't behave like one!"

We all held our breath. I really thought Rosa was going to go for her again. Instead she yelled, "You needn't think you're so ******* wonderful, Starlotta Sharman! You can't even sing in tune!"

The ******* are because Rosa said a word which probably I would not be allowed to write in a book.

Miss Marshall said, "Rosa! Starlotta! Stop this childish behaviour."

But it was too late. Rosa had gone rushing from the room.

"Dear oh dear!" said Miss Marshall. "Whatever is the matter with her?"

That was what we all wanted to know.

Chapter 3

"I tried asking her," said Dell. "Yesterday afternoon, on the way home. I said we were all dead worried about her."

"What did she say?" said Steff.

"Well, at first she jumped down my throat and said why couldn't we all mind our own business."

I groaned. Steffi said, "What is *wrong* with her?"

"That's what I said," said Dell. "I said, what's wrong with you? You do nothing but snap at people. So then she said it was just Starlotta, getting on her nerves."

"She gets on all our nerves," I said. "But we don't all go round yanking bits of her hair out."

"Even though we'd like to," said Steff.

"Yeah. Well—" Dell broke off. "Watch it! She's coming."

It seemed terrible to be talking about Rosa behind her back, but there *was* something wrong, and we all knew it. Very hastily, we changed the subject.

"I just thought of something," said Steff. "We never heard anything about that TV show we went for."

"No," I said, "and it was ages ago."

"Last week," said Rosa.

"You'd have thought we'd have heard by now."

"I bet you—" Steffi said it glumly, "I bet you it's gone to a Mona."

The Monas are what we call the people from the Mona West Academy. They wear puke yellow uniforms like dog sick and they are our deadliest rivals. They call us the Red Riding Hoods on account of our uniform being bright red. Also because in the winter we wear cloaks.

We don't take any notice of them. It would be beneath our dignity. But we hate it if they are given parts and not us!

"That woman that interviewed us," said Rosa, "she said she'd be in touch."

"They always say that. It doesn't mean anything. D'you remember the Frootie ad? They promised *faithfully* they were going to use me," I said, "and then they went and chose someone else."

"But you got the part!" cried Rosa.

"Only 'cos the other person couldn't do it."

Rosa put her thumb in her mouth and tore at her thumbnail. "They took all those pictures," she muttered.

They'd snapped away like anything. They'd taken photo after photo. But Dell said they always did that.

"It doesn't mean anything."

"And anyway, all it was, was just a couple of measly lines," said Steff. "Not a real part."

"But it's *television*," wailed Rosa. "Think of the money!"

"Wouldn't be that much." Steffi shook her head. "Not just for a couple of lines."

"It would if you got repeats," said Rosa. "Or if it sold to America."

Steffi looked at her, pityingly. "It's only the stars that get big money."

"I didn't say it would be *big*," said Rosa. "I just said it would be *money*."

"Yes, and you never know when someone might spot you," I said. "Like there might be this big-pot movie director that just happens to be watching TV and he goes, *Hey! Wow!*" I jumped up and punched the air. "*That's the girl I want for my next movie!*"

"*Holy Moly!*" Steffi couldn't resist joining in. Being spotted by hot-shot movie directors is one of our favourite games. "*That kid sure has got star quality!*"

"Da-dum, da-dum!" I made a trumpet of my hands. "The latest hot property to hit the screen...Stevie Silver and Steffi McGowran as Babes in Hollywood!"

"Movie director Stephen S—"

"Oh, stop it, can't you?" cried Rosa.

Steffi chomped on an imaginary cigar. "What's the problem, kid?"

"Just STOP IT!" screamed Rosa.

We looked at her, hurt.

"You were the one that was going on about money," I said.

"On and *on*," said Steff. "It's very vulgar, going on about money all the time."

"Money's important!"

"It may be *important*, but you don't have to go on about it. Money isn't the *only* thing."

"That's right," I said. "You don't go for auditions just for the *money*."

"Oh, get wise!" snapped Rosa.

She went stalking off across the playground.

"Just stop being such a misery!" yelled Steff.

It takes a lot to make Steffi mad. I mean, she is just not the sort to be nasty to people. All we'd been doing was have a bit of fun!

"I shall stop being friends with her," threatened Steff, "if she carries on like this."

"Nobody'll be friends with her," I said.

"No, and serve her right!"

In the middle of the lunch break, me and Rosa were called in to see Miss Todd. I always go to Miss Todd with a sinking feeling in my stomach as I am sure that I must have done something wrong. I do so many things wrong! Dancing in the street is just one example. Eating doughnuts on the tube is another. Wearing my cloak pushed off my shoulders and hanging down my back is another.

They are very strict at Starlight. You are not allowed to do *anything* that could give the school a bad name. It is because we are a stage school. We have to be extra specially well behaved or people will think, "Oh, it is those dreadful theatrical children!"

I try very hard to be well behaved, but sometimes it is difficult.

On our way to Miss Todd's office, Rosa and me discussed what we could possibly have done.

"I suppose it's Starlotta and her stupid hair," grumbled Rosa.

"*I* didn't pull her hair!" I said.

"No," said Rosa. "You just *show off* all the time."

What cheek! I don't show off. I just like to be happy.

Anyway, it wasn't either of those things. When we went into Miss Todd's office she had this great big beam stretching all the way across her face.

"Well!" she said. "Stevie and Rosa...good news! I just heard from Susie Welford."

Susie Welford! She was the casting lady; the one that had interviewed us for the parts on television.

"You've both been shortlisted. In fact, you are the *only* people to have been shortlisted. Just the two of you!"

I said, "Oh!" and beamed back at her, because I felt that was what she expected. She seemed really pleased. But to be honest, I wasn't really sure what short-listed meant!

Miss Todd explained. It meant that out of all the dozens of people who had gone for the audition, me and Rosa had been specially selected. *One* of us was going to be offered the part!

"They want you to go back tomorrow to meet the director," said Miss Todd. "Then they'll decide. Obviously you can't both be successful, but that's show business, I'm afraid. But whichever of you is lucky enough to be chosen, I want you to know that you have both done extremely well. Congratulations!"

As soon as we got back outside I said, "Wow! Just the two of us!"

I thought Rosa would be happy. I thought that at last she would cheer up and go back to being her old jokey self. I mean, we'd done better than anyone else! Including all those puke yellow Monas.

I reminded Rosa of this, but she just humped a shoulder and muttered, "We can't both get it."

"No, but at least we'll have come close," I said. "It's more than Starlotta has."

I thought that would get to her, for sure! Starlotta had done enough boasting in her time. Now Rosa could have a go.

"*And*," I added, "we'll get off classes!"

The interview was for two o'clock in the afternoon, which meant we would miss ordinary boring old school work but be back in time for Mime and Movement. I love Mime and Movement!

"Let's go back and tell the others," I said.

We wouldn't brag, because that would be like Starlotta. But there was no reason we shouldn't tell them.

"Come on!" I grabbed Rosa by the arm and tugged at her. I did so want to cheer her up! But she lagged behind me all the way along the corridor and left it to me to break the news. Starlotta, *of course*, did her usual sneering act.

"They obviously wanted little mini people that could pass for eight-year olds," she said. "I mean, I could pass for thirteen. I've grown out of baby parts."

Rosa didn't fly at her. She didn't pull her hair out. She didn't even tell her to go jump in a ditch. She just quietly walked over to her locker and started rearranging things.

Later that day I went into the cloakroom and found her hunched on top of the radiator with her arms wrapped round her legs and her knees drawn up to her chin.

She was crying.

I'd never seen Rosa cry before. She's always so bright and sparky! Not at all a crying sort of person.

Chapter 4

"Rosie, what's the matter?" I said.

Rosa just knuckled her fists and dug them into her eyes and muttered, "Nothing. Go away!"

I knew how she felt. I hate it if anyone sees me cry. People like Petal and Tiffany do it all the time, all over the place. They don't care who sees them. But I never do it in public; not if I can help it. I like to hide myself away in a secret place and be private. I guess that was what Rosa was doing. Hiding in the cloakroom and hoping no one would discover her. And I had to come blundering in! I wasn't surprised she was mad at me.

But I couldn't just go away and leave her. She was my friend.

"It'll help if you talk about it," I said.

"How do you know?" Rosa wiped her nose across her sleeve and glowered at me.

"Once when I was younger," I said, "something happened at school and I was really scared. Then Mum heard me crying in bed and asked me what the problem was."

"And you told her?"

"I talked to her about it, and after that I wasn't scared any more."

"I'm not scared!" said Rosa. And then suddenly the tears came spurting down her cheeks and she sobbed, "I believed her! I really believed her!"

"Believed who?" I said. I was bewildered. I didn't know who she was talking about.

"S-Susie Welford! The casting lady! She s-said—" Rosa hiccupped, "she said I was what she was looking for. She practically t-told me I'd g-got the p-part!"

I just couldn't think what to say. I mean, everyone knows you can't believe what they tell you at auditions. They can change their minds, or see someone else, or – well! Just anything can happen. You only believe it when you've got the contract. That's what Steffi says. It's one of the first lessons you learn. Even I had learnt it. And Rosa had been at Starlight longer than me!

But she looked so woebegone that I knew I had to say something to cheer her up. So as brightly as I could I said, "In that case, you probably *will* get the part!"

Rosa shook her head. "Not if I'm up against

you! You're the sort they want. You're cute and you're funny. I'm just *ugly*."

It really shocked me, when Rosa said that. "You're not ugly!" I told her.

"I am! My nose is too big and my teeth stick out. I look all beaky!"

It's true, in a way. Rosa does look a bit beaky. But she's so sparkling and full of life! You really don't notice.

"You went in after me," said Rosa. She scrubbed at her eyes. "They must have started having s-second thoughts!"

It is the sort of thing they do.

"But it's only a couple of lines," I reminded her. "Not like a real part."

Well. That was the wrong thing to say. It immediately set her off sobbing again.

"It mightn't be a real p-part but I need the m-money! I know you think I shouldn't talk about money but I can't help it. I've got to g-get some! 'Cos if I don't—"

Rosa scrabbled up her sleeve for a hanky and couldn't find one. I pulled a tissue out of my bag and passed it to her.

"If I don't, my mum says she's got a good mind to take me away!"

"Take you away?" I stared at her. I couldn't believe what I was hearing.

Rosa nodded, spraying tears in all directions.

"But why?" I said.

Between sobs and hiccups, Rosa told me the whole sad story. One day about two weeks ago (which was about when she had started acting strangely) Rosa had been upstairs in the bathroom washing her hands when her mum had called to her that Dell was on the telephone. Dell and Rosa had talked for ages, just like me and Steffi do. Our mums and dads can never understand it. They say, "You're at school with each other all day! What on earth do you find to talk about?" Well, of course, there are a thousand things!

"We were talking about Buster's party and what we were going to wear," sobbed Rosa.

You need to discuss these matters. It's very important, what you wear. You can't always settle it in just five minutes.

"It wasn't till I got off the phone that I realised...I'd left the water running and the plug was still in!"

"*Oh.*" I clapped a hand to my mouth. I'd done that once. It had been a DISASTER.

It had been a disaster for Rosa, as well. Water had gone all over the bathroom floor in a big lake. It had flowed out on to the landing and even started dripping its way down the stairs. The carpet had had to be taken up so that the floorboards could dry. The carpet in the bathroom had been ruined. A man had had to come in to check that the electricity was

71

all right. Another man had had to come in to check that the floors were all right. Rosa's mum and dad had had to pay out huge heaps of money that they couldn't afford and Rosa's mum was furious with her.

Blotting at her eyes, Rosa said, "She's been really ratty for ages. Even before I left the water running."

I didn't point out that Rosa had been really ratty, too. It didn't seem quite the right moment.

"She s-said I was at s-stage to school to m-make money and I'd better start making some r-really fast—" Rosa blew her noise into my tissue, "to p-pay for all the d-damage I'd done!"

"But that's the meanest thing I ever heard!" I said. "You couldn't help leaving the tap running!"

"She said it wasn't the f-first time," wept Rosa.

"You mean you'd done it before?" I said.

"Only once." Rosa sniffed. "And that was in the kitchen, where it doesn't matter."

No, 'cos kitchens are always getting wet. In any case, you couldn't ruin someone's entire life just because of a little bit of water. It was too cruel!

"What about your dad?" I said. "What's he say?"

Rosa's dad runs a sandwich bar near St Paul's Cathedral. He is ever such a jolly man. I couldn't imagine him being mean! But Rosa heaved a long, quivering sigh and said that her dad agreed with her mum.

"He said—" Rosa snatched at another tissue, "he said if I was any good I'd be appearing in commercials and earning my k-keep! He said it was about time I got something that b-brought in some m-money! He said the whole p-point of being at Starlight was they'd get you p-parts on t-telly and stuff."

I'd never looked at it like that. I mean, a part on telly would be ace! But really I'd just come to Starlight to learn how to act (and sing and dance and all the other things you need to know if you want to go into the theatrical profession).

I heard footsteps along the corridor. I said to Rosa, "Someone's coming!" and she dived into one of the toilets. Just as well, because it was Starlotta. Starlotta is the *last* person you would want to have around when you are all tear-stained and blotchy. By the time Rosa came back out, you would never have guessed she'd been crying. That is what it means to be an actor!

I squeezed her arm as we walked back down the corridor.

"I'm sure everything will be all right," I whispered. But I don't think she believed me. I wasn't sure that I did, either. I know the immense rage that parents can get in when you do something like Rosa had done. They just go, like, ballistic. Like you've done it on purpose to upset them.

Rosa hissed, "Don't tell the others," and I promised that I wouldn't.

It was really difficult, keeping it to myself. I was bursting to tell Steffi and Dell! Specially Steff, as we travelled home together on the tube. To stop myself from giving the game away, I babbled about Buster's party, instead.

"I think I shall wear my *red* leggings and my black top. The one with the swirly bits on it. What d'you reckon?"

"We discussed this already," said Steff. "I thought you'd already decided?"

"But do you think it's a good idea?" I said.

"I'll tell you what I think would be a good idea," said Steff. "I think it would be a good idea if you forgot about Buster's party and started to think about tomorrow!"

I was trying quite hard *not* to think about tomorrow. A tiny little voice somewhere inside my head kept whispering things to me. Things I didn't want to hear.

"It's only a couple of lines," I said. "Not like a real part."

I said it again to Mum, when I got home. "I've got this interview tomorrow. Me and Rosa have been short-listed."

Mum said, "Oh, Stevie, that's wonderful! How exciting! What's it for?"

"Just some boring old telly thing," I said.

Mum raised an eyebrow. "Boring old telly thing? I hope you're not getting blasé!"

"What's blarzay?" I said.

"Taking things for granted!"

"Mum, it's only a couple of *lines*," I said.

No big deal. You aren't really very likely to be spotted for the lead in someone's next Hollywood movie. That is just a game we play.

It wouldn't actually ruin my life if I wasn't chosen. But it would ruin Rosa's.

Chapter 5

When I went to bed that night I felt sure I'd lie awake for hours, tossing and turning and working myself into a state of nerves because of the interview next day. It's what I usually do before an interview. I get all wound up, like a spring.

Well! This time I didn't. I just fell asleep and stayed asleep. I didn't even dream. But things must have been going on inside my head because when I woke up next morning I found that I'd come to a decision. And I don't mean about the clothes I was going to wear to Buster's party!

I got dressed and went downstairs and found that it was Mum and Dad who were in a state of nerves. They were both really excited and wanted to wish me luck. I kept saying, "It's only a couple of lines! Not like a *real part*."

"But think how exciting!" said Mum.

"Think of the money!" urged Dad.

"It wouldn't be that much," I said. Just enough to pay for some new carpet for Rosa's mum's bathroom and make her stop being mad at Rosa. "It's only the big names that get paid fortunes."

"But what about Andrew Lloyd Webber?" said Thomas. "He could spot you for his next musical!"

Thomas knows all about the spotting game. He's heard me play it.

"Andrew Lloyd Webber wouldn't want me," I said. "I can't sing for toffee! Rosa's the one who sings."

"All right, then! What about...Orlando? What about Will?"

I blushed. He meant Orlando Bloom and Will Smith. My two most favourite movie stars!

"They wouldn't watch a boring old telly thing," I said.

Mum told me again that I was *blarzay*, and Dad said, "My! We're becoming very high and mighty."

It wasn't that at all. But I couldn't very well tell Mum and Dad what I was going to do! I couldn't tell anyone, except Rosa.

I told Rosa while we were waiting for Miss Todd to come and collect us for the interview.

"Listen," I said. "It's going to be all right!"

Rosa gave me a watery smile. She obviously thought I was just saying it to cheer her up.

"It is," I said. "Honest! I'm going to make it be."

Rosa frowned. "How d'you mean?"

"I'm going to throw it," I said.

That is an expression I have learnt since coming to Starlight. It meant that I was going to *deliberately* not get the part.

"I'm going to make them give it to you!"

Rosa's eyes grew big as soup plates. "Stevie! You can't do that!"

"Yes, I can," I said. "I can do whatever I like."

"But, Stevie!" squeaked Rosa.

"I'm your *friend*," I said. "It's what friends do."

The interview took place in Susie Welford's office, where we had been before. Only this time, as well as Susie Welford, the director was there. The director is, like, top dog. He is the one who makes the final decision. It is very important to make a good impression on the director. But I didn't want to make a good impression! I wanted Rosa to have the part. So instead of smiling politely and being suitably sort of *humble*, I stuck out my hand and said, "Hi! I'm Stevie." And the director laughed. He did! He laughed. Unfortunately, I enjoy making people laugh. I mean, it really gives me a good feeling. So when Susie handed me a sheet of paper with some words written on it and asked me to look at the camera and say them, I just sort of – well! – forgot all about poor old Rosa. I suppose you could say that I was *showing off*.

These were the words that I had to say: "When

I grow up, I'm going to be an engine driver."

And this is how I said them: "When I grow up—"
I said that bit in a silly little lispy voice like I was about
four years old, "I'm going to be an ENGINE DRIVER!"

I said the last bit in a very deep, growly, masculine
voice, and this time Susie laughed, as well as the
director. The director actually *clapped*.

It was a good thing Miss Todd wasn't in the room
with me. She is always telling us to "Just play it
straight...no funny voices." Funny voices is showing
off. But I didn't care! I love to make people laugh.

The director said, "Well! I'm not sure I'd want to
go anywhere in a train that was driven by you,
young lady!"

I said, "Why not?" Just as cheekily as I dared.
"Women can drive trains just as well as men."

The director said, "Oh! So you're a feminist, are
you? Well, it suits the part. Wouldn't you say so,
Susie?"

Susie nodded and said, "Absolutely!"

As I left, the director shook hands with me and
said, "It's been a pleasure! I'm sure our paths will
cross again."

Susie came over to the door to see me off. "The
director was very impressed," she whispered. Then
she winked at me and said, "Nice performance! We'll
be in touch."

I was walking on air – until I got back to the

reception area and saw Rosa. Then I felt terrible. What had I done??? I'd promised her that she could have the part!

As we left the building, Miss Todd asked us how we'd got on. Rosa grew a bit pink and said, "Quite well, I think."

"Stevie?" said Miss Todd. "How about you?"

I mumbled, "I don't know. Not sure."

"That doesn't sound too hopeful," said Miss Todd. "Never mind! There'll be plenty more opportunities."

Rosa gave me this *look*, and I just nearly died.

I felt bad all the rest of the day. On the way home Steffi said, "So what do you think? Do you think you've got it?" Then I got home and it was Mum who wanted to know, then Thomas, then Dad. I didn't know what to say! It had been a really good interview and I felt sure that I probably had got it. But I'd meant for it to go to Rosa! She was my friend, and I'd let her down. I just felt so ashamed! I'd been so busy showing off that I'd completely forgotten my promise.

That night I stayed awake *all night long*. I just couldn't think how I was going to face Rosa. Susie had as good as promised me the part. What was I going to say???

Next morning I met Steffi as usual and we travelled in to school together.

"Today's the big day!" sang Steff. "Today's the day

you'll know if you've got it!"

"I think I have," I said.

"Well! That's pushing your luck," said Steff.

"I know." I fiddled miserably with the strap on my school bag. "It's just something I feel."

"You don't exactly sound overjoyed about it!"

"I just feel so sorry for Rosa," I said.

"Oh, Stevie, you can't *afford* to!" said Steff. "You have to be tough, in this business!"

It's what she's always telling me: you have to be tough, if you want to survive. And I am going to do more than just survive. I am going to be a S*T*A*R*! That still didn't stop me feeling dreadful about Rosa.

At first break I had to go to the office about some lost property. I am always losing things! Steffi says I would lose my head if it wasn't stuck on to my shoulders. When I went back into the yard, Rosa wasn't there. I was about to ask where she'd gone when she came flying towards us.

"Guess what?" she cried. "I've got it!"

"The telly thing?" said Dell.

Rosa nodded. She was all flushed and beaming. Steffi shot this little worried glance at me.

"Rosa, that is *wonderful*!" I said.

There was one bit of me that really meant it. It was wonderful. Now Rosa's mum and dad wouldn't be mad at her any more! It was what I'd wanted.

But there was another bit of me, a mean little twizzly bit, that felt really outraged. How could they have given the part to Rosa instead of me? I'd made them laugh! The director had clapped me! He had been impressed. *Why choose Rosa and not me*?

Later, in the lunch break, Rosa tugged me off to a quiet corner of the yard, behind the kitchens, where we wouldn't be interrupted. She wanted to thank me.

"It's awful," she said, "'cos last night my mum apologised to me for being so ratty. She said she hadn't meant to be but she's been feeling really rough these last few weeks. Guess why?"

"Dunno," I said.

"She's having babies!" said Rosa.

"*Babies*?" I said.

"Twins!" said Rosa. "She's only just discovered!"

"Blimey," I said. I thought that in that case it was just as well Rosa had got the part. I mean, *twins*! You'd have to buy two of everything. "I bet she's even more ratty, now," I said.

"No!" Rosa's eyes were shining. "She's dead excited! So'm I. So's my dad!"

Weird. Rosa's already got two little brothers and an older sister. But I guess some people just really like having babies.

"She told me it didn't matter whether I got the part or not," said Rosa. "She said *of course* she wouldn't take me away. But now I just feel so horribly guilty!

If it wasn't for me, you could have had it!"

I didn't know whether to say anything or not. I didn't *want* to say anything. But I couldn't let Rosa go on feeling guilty.

So I told her.

What else could I do? She is my friend! And I still had the satisfaction of knowing that the director had been impressed. One of these days he'd use me! The next time he wanted a good laugh...

Stevie Silver
Star Struck

Chapter 1

STEVIE SILVER
S*U*P*E*R*S*T*A*R*

I write this everywhere! All over the place. In my school books, in my diary. Even on my bedroom wall! I am not just going to be a S*T*A*R*, I am going to be a S*U*P*E*R*S*T*A*R*. It is my big ambition in life.

So you can imagine how I felt when one day my mum told me that I was going to have to leave stage school. I couldn't believe it! Leave Starlight? It had to be some kind of bad dream!

But it wasn't a dream; it was a horrid reality. Mum explained to me how Dad's business had been doing badly and he was going to have to close it down and find some other kind of job. If he could. Mum didn't seem too hopeful.

"You see, Stevie, your dad's not a young man any more. He's over forty. There aren't that many jobs for older people."

I could see that being over forty made you pretty ancient. But Mum wasn't over forty!

"You're still young," I told her. "You could get a job!"

Mum said that she was certainly going to look for one.

"But even if we both manage to find something, I'm afraid there still won't be enough money to pay your fees at Starlight. It costs a lot to send you to a stage school."

"You could use the money I earned from the Frooties ad!" I said.

I'd done this commercial a little while ago and Mum and Dad had made me put all the money in the building society for when I was older. But why wait till I was older? I needed it now, so I could stay on at Starlight!

But Mum shook her head and said that what I'd earned from the Frooties ad would only be enough for just one term.

"So I could stay on for next term, at least," I said. "And then maybe I'd get another ad, and then another one, and—"

"Stevie, I'm sorry. It would just put too much pressure on you," said Mum. "And in the long run, it would only make things worse. Better leave now, at the end of the school year. It won't be so bad! You can go to The Chase and meet up again with all your old friends from primary school."

I didn't want to meet up with my friends from primary school! I didn't want to go to The Chase! The Chase is an ordinary *boring* sort of school. They don't do Mime, or Voice, or Movement. They don't send you for auditions. How could I be a superstar if I went to The Chase?

Mum said soothingly that maybe when I finished school I would be able to go somewhere like the Royal Academy of Dramatic Art and study. And in the meantime, perhaps, Dad would let me use my building society money to pay for acting classes on a Saturday morning.

"That's no good!" I roared.

It would be years and *years* before I finished school. By that time all my friends from Starlight, Dell and Steffi and Rosa, would be real professionals, working in the business. They would be in musicals, they would be on television, they would be going off on tour. Oh, I couldn't bear it!

Mum said again about classes on a Saturday morning. But it wouldn't be the same! Classes on a Saturday were for amateurs. People who were just doing it for fun. I was serious!

"Stevie, I'm so sorry," said Mum. "I know how much it means to you."

"You don't!" I sobbed. "You can't possibly!"

"Sweetheart, I do! Your dad and I both feel terrible about it. Unfortunately, it's just one of those things."

"But it's not fair!"

"Life isn't always fair," said Mum. "Think of all those children who can't even go to Saturday morning classes."

I didn't care about them. I only cared about me! Mum sighed and said that it was going to be hard for all of us.

"Especially your dad. So please, Stevie! Try to be brave. I don't want you making your dad feel worse than he already does."

I felt like screaming, "Never mind Dad! What about me?"

"My entire life is going to be ruined," I told Mum. And I ran upstairs to my bedroom and slammed the door behind me. "I might as well be dead!"

I threw myself on to my bed and buried my head in the pillow. How could I go back to an ordinary school after being at Starlight? Starlight made me feel so special! I loved walking down the road with Steff to catch the tube every morning. I loved everyone knowing that we were stage school students. I just loved everything about it! The tap shoes, the ballet shoes, the leotards, the greasepaint – everything!

I suddenly remembered Rosa, last term. Her mum had told her that *she* was going to have to leave.

I'd felt so sorry for her! I'd never dreamt that the very same thing would soon be happening to me...

Tears went squelching into my pillow. Rosa's mum had been mad at her because she'd left a tap running in the bathroom and practically flooded the house. That was why Rosa was going to have to leave. But I hadn't left any taps running! I hadn't done anything. It was all so unfair!

Rosa's mum had forgiven her, in the end. She'd discovered she was having a baby – *two* babies, in fact! She was having *twins*. It had made her so happy she'd told Rosa she could stay.

I couldn't see my mum suddenly discovering she was having twins and being happy about it. Not if Dad was going to be out of work and we didn't have any money.

My life was falling to pieces and there was nothing I could do about it!

I heard footsteps thudding up the stairs. My brother, Thomas. He always thuds and bangs. Next thing I knew, he was hammering on my door.

"Hey, Stevie!"

"Go away!" I snarled.

"But I want to talk to you!"

"Well, I don't want to talk to you. Just go away!" I flipped over on to my back and smothered my face with the pillow. "Gowaylivlone!"

"You what?" said Thomas.

I screamed and sprang into a sitting position. I shouted, "Go boil yourself, frog face!" and hurled my pillow at the door. Sheba, one of our cats, had been peacefully sleeping at the end of my bed. She fled with a yowl of fright as the pillow went flumping past her.

That made me feel mean. My life might have been shattered beyond all hope of repair, but I didn't have to take it out on a poor little innocent cat.

"You still there?" said Thomas, from the other side of the door.

I felt like screaming, "Where d'you think I am? Outer space?" But I was suddenly remembering Rosa again. We'd all been so worried about her. We couldn't understand why she was being so ratty with everyone. Now I was being ratty with Thomas. And frightening poor Sheba! So I didn't scream. Instead, I found a tissue and blotted at my eyes and muttered, "You can come in if you must."

Thomas pushed the door open just the tiniest crack and sort of slinked his way through. He has no idea how to make an entrance! He'll never be an actor. But that's all right 'cos he doesn't want to be. Thomas is the brains of the family, I am the creative one.

Thomas mumbled, "Mum just told me."

I didn't say anything; I couldn't. I knew if I tried I'd start crying all over again, and I just hate crying in front of people.

"I'm sorry," said Thomas, gruffly. "I wish there was something I could do."

"Well, there isn't." I didn't mean to say it so ungraciously. It just came out that way.

Thomas frowned. He scooped up Sheba, who was mewing piteously round his legs. Telling him how horrid I'd been to her!

"I know it sounds like your life has come to an end," he said, "but you'll still be a star!"

I sniffed, dolefully. "How d'you know?"

"'Cos I know," said Thomas. "It's what Auntie Lily says...if you've got what it takes, you'll get there! And you have," said Thomas. "So you will!"

Chapter 2

There are times when I feel like bashing and hashing at Thomas. Times when I could cheerfully *mash him to a pulp.*

There are other times when I think he is the very best brother in the whole world.

It really made me glow, him saying that I had what it takes! I went away and wrote STEVIE SILVER S*U*P*E*R*S*T*A*R* over everything I could find, including the chalk board that Mum keeps in the kitchen for making shopping lists on.

"That's the spirit!" said Mum. "After all, think of all those big names who've never been to a drama school in their life!"

"Which ones?" I said. But of course Mum couldn't think of a single solitary person, could she?

Dad, trying to cheer me up, said that nobody could teach you how to act. "You've either got it or you haven't."

"And we all agree that you *have*," said Mum.

I went to bed feeling a bit better and determined that I would make it to the top *no matter what*. I would do what Mum said and go to Saturday morning classes, and I would be the S*T*A*R* because of having been to stage school and being serious about it, and one day (when I'd been there about six months) they would put on a show and a top movie director would come and see it and – Hey Presto! Bingo! Wham! That would be *it*. I'd be whizzed off to Hollywood and given a whopping big contract worth millions of dollars. We would all be rich as could be and Dad would never have to worry about working ever again.

Unfortunately, when I woke up in the morning it all seemed like a silly childish daydream. No one was going to whizz me off to Hollywood. I would be left to moulder at a boring ordinary school doing boring ordinary lessons and every time I looked at the television and saw someone my own age I would feel like howling. I would just be so *jealous*. I would be *green*. Especially if it was Starlotta.

Starlotta was a girl in my class at Starlight. She thought she was the cat's whiskers. The fairy on the Christmas tree. The icing on the cake. All because she had an uncle that was in a TV soap. I couldn't bear for Starlotta to know that my dad had lost all his money and I was going to leave!

I met Steffi as usual and we walked to the tube station. Steff couldn't understand why I was so glum.

"Do cheer up!" she said. "You look as if you've just been up for the lead part and been given the understudy!"

I tried not to snap at her, because after all it wasn't her fault. I heaved a sigh and said, "I've got something to tell you."

"What?"

"Not now," I said. "Later."

Rosa had hugged her terrible secret to herself for ages. It wasn't till I'd found her crying in the cloakroom one day that I'd discovered what was wrong. I'd told her that talking about it would help. Now it was me that had the same terrible secret, and I wasn't sure that talking would help. But Steffi is my best friend. I couldn't keep it from her.

It was raining at first break and we were allowed to stay in school. We were *supposed* to stay in the hall or in our classrooms, but I whispered to Steff to come down to the cloakroom.

"What about the others?" she said.

I hesitated, then said, "Yes, all right. Them too."

We were all friends – me and Steff, Dell and Rosa. Friends are meant to share. Bad things as well as good.

We scuttled down to the cloakroom, making sure that no one saw us. We are not really allowed to sit about down there. I don't know why; in case there's a fire or something, maybe. They like to know where people are. Anyway, it's where we always go if we want to be secret.

Rosa perched on one of the wash basins, Dell and Steffi sat on a hot water pipe. I scrunched myself up on the windowsill, hugging my knees to my chin just like Rosa had, the day I found her crying.

"Stevie's got something to tell us," said Steff.

Rosa took one look at my face and moaned, "Oh, no! Your parents are emigrating!"

She said this because one of her cousins had just gone to Australia. Now she expected everybody to be going there!

"Why always think the worst?" said Dell. "It could be something nice!"

"Yes, like she's suddenly been offered this fabulous part on telly," said Steff.

She looked at me, hopefully, but I slowly shook my head. They all sat there, waiting for me to say something. I gulped, took a deep, deep breath and let it all come out.

"My dad's shut down his business 'cos it's not making any money and it means I've got to leave!"

There was a shocked silence.

"Stevie, *no!*" cried Steff.

"You can't!" wailed Rosa.

"This is really serious," said Dell.

97

"I know." I hiccupped, miserably. "It's the worst thing that's ever happened to me."

"Maybe," said Steff, "they'll change their minds?"

"Like mine did," said Rosa.

"Maybe your dad could start a different sort of business," suggested Dell.

"Yes, or go and work for someone else," said Steff.

"I don't think so," I said. "He's too old...he's over forty."

A curtain of black gloom descended upon us.

"How about—" Rosa brightened, "how about he came and helped my dad in his sandwich bar?"

"He doesn't know anything about sandwiches," I said. "He can't even boil an egg. That's what my mum says."

"There's got to be something," said Steff. "You can't leave Starlight!"

I blinked, and tilted my chin a bit higher so the tears couldn't drip off.

"Dad's already written a letter...he's told Miss Todd they're taking me away at the end of this term."

"This is just *awful*!" yelped Steff.

"I can't bear it!" said Rosa.

"We're the Gang of Four," said Dell.

It is a great comfort to have friends who care about you, but there wasn't anything, alas, that they could actually do. It wasn't like when we'd raised money to help the poor cats of Cats' Cottage when they ran out of funds. We couldn't *ever* raise enough money to pay for my school fees.

The bell rang for the end of break and we all dismally peeled ourselves away from the hot water pipes and the wash basin and the windowsill and trailed back out into the corridor. We had walked as far as the stairs that led up to our classroom when I heard a door bang. I turned and saw Starlotta coming out of the cloakroom. She had been there all the time! Hiding behind a row of pegs, or shut away behind a door. She must have heard everything we'd said!

"How low can you sink?" said Steff.

Rosa sniffed. "Only what you'd expect of her."

Rosa couldn't stand Starlotta. None of us really liked her. I absolutely *hated* the thought of her knowing about me having to leave Starlight.

"I bet she goes and tells everyone," I said. "I bet she gloats!"

But she didn't. She didn't say a word! I was really amazed. I mean, gloating is what she loves best. Of course she would have to admit she'd been eavesdropping, but she'd have found a way to do it.

"I'm *sooo* sorry, Stevie! I couldn't help overhearing. How simply terrible for you! I would just die if I had to leave."

That's the sort of thing I would have expected. Instead, she just gave me this strange little pale smile. Well, her face was pale. The smile was little. And strange. What was she smiling at me for? It was like she was saying, "Don't worry! Your secret is safe with me."

Really weird.

And then, the next day, all was revealed. I discovered why she hadn't gloated.

First thing after lunch I was called to see Miss Todd. I'm usually a bit apprehensive when I go and see Miss Todd as I am always wondering to myself what I have done wrong. This time I knew that I hadn't done anything wrong. She was calling me in because of Dad's letter.

"Stevie," she said. "Take a seat! I was sorry to hear that you might have to be leaving us."

Might have to be? My ears pricked up.

"I wonder," said Miss Todd, "if you've considered trying for a scholarship?"

Well! It was the first I'd ever heard of a scholarship.

"The British Drama Foundation awards one scholarship a year to every school that's a member. I'd be very happy to put you in for it, if you think your parents would agree."

"They would!" I said.

They had to! It was my only chance.

"I'll discuss the details with them," said Miss Todd. "There's only one other candidate from the school, and that's Starlotta."

Starlotta??? I think my jaw must have dropped open, or maybe I looked like a person that's had a ton of bricks dropped on their head.

"I know only one of you can be successful," said Miss Todd, "but I do think it's worth a go. After all—" she smiled at me, "what have you got to lose?"

"N-nothing," I stammered.

"Exactly!" said Miss Todd. "Nothing to lose, and everything to gain. Off you go! I'll have a word with your parents.

I left Miss Todd's office and went racing back down the corridor. I couldn't wait to tell the others! I was going to try for a scholarship!

Yes, and so was Starlotta...

Chapter 3

"*Starlotta*?" said Rosa. "What does she need a scholarship for?"

I'd told them about it as I didn't think it was a secret. I mean, Miss Todd hadn't said not to tell people. And everyone was going to know about me! Now that I was trying for a scholarship, I didn't mind who got to hear of it.

"*Her* dad isn't out of work," said Rosa, "is he?"

"She hasn't got a dad," said Steffi. "Her mum's divorced."

There was a bit of a silence at this. The rest of us had not realised Starlotta hadn't got a dad. Then Rosa muttered, "Not surprised her mum's divorced if she's anything like Starlotta. Who'd want to live with it?"

"And anyway," said Dell, "what about her uncle?"

Starlotta's famous uncle that was on the telly. Why

couldn't he pay for her?

"He must be rich as rich," I said.

"Rolling in it," said Rosa.

"I'm sure if Auntie Lily was rich, she'd pay for me," I said.

Unfortunately, my Auntie Lily doesn't have any money. She always says she never had the knack of making it. Whenever she gets any, like if a little checky-poo arrives (checky-poo is what she calls a cheque) she immediately puts it in her knickers for fear of losing it. She is a little bit peculiar, but she is my very favourite auntie.

"Are you sure she wouldn't pay?" said Steffi, later, as we travelled home on the tube.

"She couldn't afford to," I said. "She is permanently brassic."

Brassic is what Auntie Lily says when she means broke. When she doesn't have a *bean*.

Steffi sighed. "It is such a nuisance! Why does Starlotta's uncle have to be so stingy?"

I knew what she was trying to say. She was trying to say that if only Starlotta's uncle would pay for her, Starlotta wouldn't have to compete with me for a scholarship. And if Starlotta wasn't competing, I would stand a far better chance of getting one.

I mean, it wouldn't be absolutely certain, because I would still have to convince the judges I was worthy of it; but at least I wouldn't have to convince them that I was more worthy than Starlotta!

"Maybe," I suggested, "her uncle doesn't really like her?"

"Who does?" muttered Steff. "Maybe he just doesn't think she's good enough?"

There was a pause, while we thought about it.

"But she is," I said, "isn't she?"

"No better than you!" Steff turned on me, fiercely. "Don't go thinking she's better than you, just 'cos of her uncle and her big loud mouth!"

Steffi is my friend and incredibly loyal. But all the same, I knew that Starlotta *was* good. I'd never liked her very much, and now she was sort of – well! – my enemy, almost. But it was no use pretending she hadn't "got what it takes".

The more I thought about it, the more depressed I became. How could I hope to get a scholarship when I was up against Starlotta? She is everything that I am not! She is tall and I am short: she is blond and I am mouse. I have freckles and a silly little round face with sticky-out ears like a pixie. Starlotta is all peaches-and-cream, with *blue* eyes and a dead straight nose. My nose is short and blobby, like it was stuck on as some kind of afterthought. Like a lump of Play-Doh. I hate my nose!

I'd once tried sticking it down with Sellotape when I went to bed at night, but all that happened was my face got sore. My nose was just as short and blobby as ever.

Who was going to give a scholarship to someone with a blobby nose?

The others did their best to make me feel better.

Dell said that I must "think positively". Rosa said that Miss Todd wouldn't have put me in for the scholarship if she didn't reckon I stood a chance. Steffi said that Starlotta might be talented but she had a lousy personality. She said, "You are all bright and bubbly. And you are *funny*. Starlotta loves herself too much."

"Yes, and anyway, there are loads of Starlotta look-alikes out there," said Rosa. "You're the only one that looks like you!"

"Which is what they want," said Dell. "Somebody *different*."

Unfortunately, instead of making me feel better, it all just made me feel worse! I knew they were only saying these things because they were worried that really I didn't stand a chance.

The scholarship auditions were arranged for half term. They were to be held in an old mansion way out in the country. The mansion had been turned into a drama school, where people went as boarders.

I thought how romantic it must be, and just for a moment I wished that I could be a boarder. But then I thought of Starlight and how happy I was there, and how exciting it was to be right in the middle of London, surrounded by theatres. And a great lump rose up in my throat and wouldn't go away, no matter how hard I swallowed. I couldn't bear to leave Starlight!

Miss Todd had sent all the details to Mum and Dad, including the time of my audition and a map of how to get there. Mum said she would take a day off from helping Dad pack up the office and would drive me down.

Then I had a real surprise. Well! More of a nasty shock, I suppose you would say. Starlotta came up to me one morning and asked if Mum would take her to the audition, as well. I was, like, flabbergasted. *Starlotta*? Travelling with us?

"My mum hasn't got a car," she said. "And it's a really long journey by train."

I felt like saying, "So what? It's not my problem if your mum hasn't got a car." But she was being almost humble. I'd never known Starlotta be humble before! I guess it threw me. I mumbled, "I'll ask my mum."

"You idiot!" screamed Steffi when I told her about it. "You don't want to travel down with her, yacking on at you all the time!"

I didn't. It was the very last thing I wanted.

"You're too soft," grumbled Steff. "You should have told her to go by train. Then she might have got lost and never turned up. Tee hee! Serve her right!"

"Slow on the uptake," said Rosa; and she nodded severely and tapped a finger to her forehead. "You need your head examined!"

That's what I thought, too. I asked Mum, like I'd promised, and I really hoped she'd say that it was too much bother, or the car was going to be full of boxes (from Dad's office). Of course she didn't.

"That's a good idea," she said. "You'll be company for each other."

"Mum!" I shrieked. "It's Starlotta!"

"You mean, you'd rather she didn't come with us?" said Mum.

"I can't stand her!"

"So why did you ask?"

"I dunno." I hunched a shoulder. "Felt sorry for her, I s'pose."

"And now you want me to do your dirty work for you and say no. Is that it?"

I hunched my other shoulder and muttered again that I didn't know.

"Look," said Mum, "there's no law that says we have to take her. But it would seem a bit unkind not to. Don't you think?"

I heaved a sigh. "I guess."

"She can sit in the back," said Mum. "You don't have to talk. You can tell her you want to be quiet and prepare for the audition. She'll probably want to be quiet, too."

Huh! Mum didn't know Starlotta. Her and her big mouth! She'd be clacking all the way there.

Chapter 4

Rosa was right. I needed my head examined!

The day of the audition arrived and everyone, but everyone, had sent me good luck cards. Steffi, Dell, Rosa, both my nans and granddads, Auntie Lily, Mum and Dad – even Thomas. It was lovely of them, but it didn't half make me nervous! There were all these people wanting so desperately for me to do well, and here was I, shaking in my shoes before I'd even got there.

I was! I was shaking! Mum had to come and calm me down.

Thomas said, "Give her a slug of Dad's whisky. *I* would!"

But Mum said, "She's going to be all right. She's going to take a *deep* breath and count very *slooooooowly* up to ten and tell herself that she is going to be a STAR, no matter what!"

Even Mum was at it, now. I just *had* to get that scholarship!

Miss Todd had told us to wear clothes that we felt comfortable in, not clothes that looked good but were too tight or made us hot and bothered or would get all creased from sitting in the car. She said, "You need to be as relaxed as you can."

Mum asked me what I'd feel happiest in, so I said, "Jeans and T-shirt." At which Mum raised her eyebrows! But she said I could wear just whatever I liked. I didn't have to wear a dress if I didn't want.

I didn't. But Starlotta did! Wouldn't you know it? She turned up at our place all got up like a dog's dinner. She'd even got blue sparkly stuff on her eyes! I immediately felt childish and dowdy and wished I could go back and change, but it was too late. We didn't have time. I was sure I caught Starlotta looking at me with a satisfied smirk on her face. I bet I knew what she was thinking: Stevie Silver is just *sooo* babyish!

I thought gloomily that she was probably right and that I *was* rather babyish. But at least I could make people laugh! I do it without even meaning to. I just say things, perfectly ordinary things, and they start falling about.

Starlotta never makes people laugh. She just

makes them gnash their teeth and want to bop her one.

And of course she couldn't sit in the back of the car and be quiet, could she? Oh, no! The big blabbermouth started blabbering the minute Mum pulled away from the kerb. All about what a dear little car we had, it was just *sooo* sweet!

"My uncle has a really big one. He calls it his gas guzzler. You can get ten people in his car."

"My goodness!" said Mum. "What a pity he couldn't have you driven you down in it today."

"Oh, he couldn't," said Starlotta. "He's busy. He's filming."

"Mum's busy, too," I said.

"It is *sooo* nice of you to give me a lift," gushed Starlotta.

She can really put it on when she wants to. She opens her eyes very wide and sort of *bats* at you with her eyelashes. Mum didn't seem terribly impressed. She seemed more amused than anything.

"Please don't mention it," she told Starlotta. "I'm sure—"

Quite suddenly, without any warning, Mum broke off and swung the wheel hard to the right. Fortunately there was nothing coming towards us. I guess she wouldn't have done if it there had been, and then—

But I don't like to think about that.

"*Mum!*" I shrieked. "Stop!"

"Yes, I see it," said Mum.

"What, what?" cried Starlotta.

"A cat!" I was out of the door and racing back the way we had come even before the car had properly stopped moving. Lying in the road was the sweetest kitten you have ever seen. The colour of apricots, with a snow-white bib and little black tips to its paws. I couldn't see anything horrid like blood, but the poor little thing wasn't moving. Mum came running to join me.

"It's still breathing," she said. "Quick, Stevie! Run and get a rug from the car."

"What's happening?" demanded Starlotta, as I wrenched open the rear passenger door and yanked at the rug she was sitting on.

"Gimme!" I panted.

"Why? What? What's going on?"

"Just GET OFF!" I roared.

I snatched at the rug and went tearing back to Mum.

"Poor little soul," she said. "It's far too young to be out! Let's roll it very gently on to the rug...gently! That's it."

We all love cats in our family. Well, we love all animals, but cats are our special thing. We would have dozens if we lived in the country!

Mum and I carried the little injured kitten ever so carefully back to the car. We couldn't find any marks

111

on it and Mum said she just hoped it didn't have any dreadful damage inside, where we couldn't see.

"What do we do?" I whispered.

"Well…" Mum paused. She looked from me to Starlotta. "It obviously needs to be taken to the vet just as soon as possible."

"Then let's take it!" I said.

"What, *now*?" Starlotta sounded indignant. "We've got an audition to go to!"

"But it's hurt," I said. "It could die!"

"Yes, and we could be late! You know what Miss Todd says about being late."

I chewed rather hard at my thumb nail. To be late for an audition is one of the very worst crimes you can commit. But a little cat's life was at stake! Thomas would never forgive me.

I would never forgive me.

"Well, girls, we have to decide," said Mum. "What do we do? Do we go on or turn back?"

Go on! Turn back!

Starlotta and I shouted it together. I bounced round in my seat. "The vet is only just up the road!"

"But we haven't got time!" roared Starlotta. "We'll miss the audition!"

"Stevie?" Mum was still cradling the kitten. "It's your decision."

"Why hers?" screeched Starlotta. "She can miss the audition if she wants. I don't see why I should!"

"Starlotta, I'm really sorry," said Mum, "but I can't do what both of you want...I can't turn back *and* go on. I'm only saying it's Stevie's decision because— well! You did ask to come with us. If you weren't here, then Stevie would be free to choose."

"I'm a guest in your car!" yelled Starlotta.

"Yes," said Mum, "and a guest usually follows the house rules. Now, Stevie, come on! What do you want us to do?"

I said, "Take it to the vet, Mum. Please!"

We turned the car round and headed back to the vet, with Starlotta sulking all the way. The vet took the kitten in immediately and promised to do his best for it.

"Please don't worry about the expense," said Mum.

"No," I said, "'cos I've got my building society money!"

Starlotta gave me a look of deepest hate as we got back in the car.

"Well, that's it," she said. "We've missed it now."

Mum drove as fast as she could without breaking any speed limits – Mum is ever such a careful driver. Dad says she drives a car as if it's a baby buggy – but there was just no way we were going to get to that audition on time.

Starlotta sat in the back and scowled. She said the kitten would probably die anyway and we would have ruined our chances for nothing. She said if you wanted to *get* somewhere and *be* someone, you couldn't afford to be sentimental.

"You have to be single-minded! You have to want something *so badly* you won't let anything stand in your way."

Mum said, "Wouldn't that make you rather hard and unfeeling? You might get to be a star, but I don't think you'd be a very nice person."

That shut her up! But I knew she was thinking to herself that she had got what it takes and I hadn't.

Was it really true that I wasn't single-minded enough?

Chapter 5

We arrived for the audition almost twenty minutes late. Starlotta was in the hugest sulk ever. She was in an absolute *mega* sulk. She hadn't even opened her mouth for the last few miles!

"Don't worry," promised Mum. "I'll tell them what happened."

But Starlotta couldn't wait for Mum. She went charging out of the car and racing ahead of us up the steps. By the time Mum and me caught up with her, she was already babbling out the story to a lady at the reception desk.

"They stopped to take this cat to the vet! It wasn't my fault. I told them we'd be late!"

"Yes, she did," said Mum. "It wasn't the girls' fault. If anyone's, it was mine."

The reception lady said that she would "Go and talk to Mr Barnaby and find out whether he'll see you."

She didn't sound terribly hopeful.

Mum and me and Starlotta all sat in a row in the hall. I chewed my nails while Starlotta practised smiling and tried to pretend that she wasn't with us. I whispered to Mum that it hadn't really been her fault, it had been mine; but Mum just squeezed my hand and said, "Nonsense! I was the one at the wheel."

It was a comfort to know that Mum was on my side, but I could understand why Starlotta was in such a rage. Not everyone feels about animals the way me and my family do.

After what seemed like forever, the reception lady came back.

"You're lucky," she said. "Mr Barnaby's agreed to see you."

Whew! What a relief! I looked at Starlotta and grinned, but she only tossed her head and made a sniffing sound.

Because her surname is Sharman and mine is Silver, Starlotta went in for her interview before me. (First we had the interview, then we had the audition.) Starlotta was in there for about ten minutes, and when she came out she was smiling. A *real* smile. Not one of her pretend ones that she does in case someone walks by with a camera. She was happy!

I might as well admit it: my heart *sank*. If Starlotta

was happy, it meant her interview had gone well. Mr Barnaby had obviously liked her. He had obviously been impressed by her.

I tried to remind myself that I was me and I could make people laugh.

But I didn't make Mr Barnaby laugh. He wasn't a laughing sort of person. He was very long and thin with a long thin face, all dismal and melancholy, and hands that had the most enormous knuckles. I kept staring at his knuckles all the time he was talking. I couldn't help it! He kept cracking them. They went off like pop guns. Pop! Crack! Click! I half expected them to start firing missiles.

Mr Barnaby wanted to know what experience I'd had, and what I most enjoyed about being at Starlight, and which classes I was best at.

I told him about the Frooties ad and the time I'd danced the Rag Doll in a Christmas show when my best friend Steffi had had appendicitis.

I said that what I enjoyed most about Starlight was being with other people who had the same ambitions as me, and that the classes I was best at were Mime and Movement (but not Ballet!) and "being funny and doing impersonations, only we don't actually have classes in that."

Mr Barnaby said, "I see," and cracked all his knuckles – pop, pop, pop! – one after another. "So you're a comedian?"

I told him that I didn't mean to be. "It just seems to happen. I say things that I think are quite normal and people start to laugh."

Mr Barnaby didn't laugh. He didn't laugh *at all*. He just asked me if I could do one of my impersonations for him, so I did Miss Todd being cross with us and he didn't even smile.

"Why do you want to be an actor?" he said.

By now I was feeling really depressed because this interview was *not* going well. But then I remembered something that Miss Todd had once said to us.

"All audiences are different. Some will laugh, some will cry. Some won't do anything at all. Whatever happens, you mustn't let it throw you. Just keep going, and do your best."

So when Mr Barnaby asked me why I wanted to be an actor, I dragged my gaze away from his knuckles and looked him straight in the eye and said, "'Cos it's the only thing I can imagine being. It's the only thing I *want* to be. I like it when people laugh, it makes me feel good. And it makes them feel good, too!" I added.

He still didn't smile. He said, "Right, well, I think the time has come for some action."

He led me down a long corridor and up some steps, and suddenly I found myself on stage! I could see there were some people out front. One of them came over to the footlights and said, "Hallo! Stevie, isn't it? I'm Mrs James. I'm just going to ask you and your friend to do a little improvisation for us."

Me and my friend? What friend? I stared round in panic. Surely she didn't mean Starlotta???

She did! Fresh gloom descended upon me as Starlotta came bounding out on to the stage. Mrs James said, "Now, you both know what I mean by improvisation, I hope?"

We nodded. We sometimes did Impro (that was what we called it) at Starlight. Miss Todd would tell us to act out a scene "in your own words". I usually enjoyed it – but not with Starlotta!

I don't think she was too pleased, either. I don't think she'd been expecting anything like this.

But worse was to come...I nearly sank through the floor when Mrs James told us what she wanted us to do. She wanted us to act out the scene in the car, when me and Starlotta were arguing about whether to turn back or go on.

I just knew, then, that that was *it*. I wasn't going to get that scholarship.

Starlotta gave me this little superior smirk. We arranged two chairs, one behind the other, and I sat in the front one and Starlotta sat at the back (but making sure the audience could see her. She is not stupid).

This is how some of our dialogue went:

Me: *It could die if we don't get it to the vet!*

Starlotta: *Yes, and I could miss my chance for a scholarship if we don't get to the audition!*

Me: *But we can't just leave it!*

Starlotta: *Look, if you want to miss the audition, that's up to you.*

Me: *I don't want to miss it!*

Starlotta: *Well, you will, and so will I, and then I'll never forgive you! I want to be an actor more than anything else on earth! I am SINGLE–MINDED! I'll do ANYTHING to get there!*

It was like we were having a battle, and Starlotta was scoring all the points. She was really full of herself on the way home. She talked practically *non-stop.*

When Dad and Thomas asked me how the audition had gone, I told them that it had been disastrous. Dad said, "Oh, come on! I'm sure it wasn't."

Thomas said, "Well, even if it was, at least you rescued a cat."

Mum had rung up the vet and the vet had said the kitten was going to be "just fine". Mum had promised that if no one claimed it, we could have it for our own. I tried really hard to be pleased. I mean, I was pleased. But all the same, I felt that my life had come to an end.

Chapter 6

The day the letter came, Mum was out. She was helping Dad in the office and me and Thomas were in the house alone. I was in the kitchen feeding the cats when Thomas came rushing at me, excitedly waving an envelope.

"It's from the scholarship people!"

I snatched it from him. "How do you know?"

"Says on it...British Drama Foundation. Open it, quick!"

I was so scared, I almost didn't want to. My fingers were all trembly. I had to force myself.

It was a very large envelope with a whole wodge of stuff inside it. I pulled everything out. On top was a letter, held in place by a red paper clip. I took one look, and all the blood in my veins just turned to a mush.

> We regret to inform you that we
> do not feel able to offer you a
> scholarship on this occasion

"What? What is it?" said Thomas.

I couldn't speak. I just choked and thrust the letter at him, then turned and ran from the room.

I headed for my bedroom, which is where I always go when I want to cry. Seconds later I heard Thomas thudding up the stairs behind me. I knew he only wanted to tell me how sorry he was, but I just couldn't bear it.

"Please, Thomas, go away!" I said.

"But Stevie—" The door came crashing open and Thomas galloped through. We *never* go into each other's bedrooms without being invited. "Stevie, you've got it! Look!"

He waved a sheet of paper at me. I looked – and couldn't believe my eyes!

> Dear Stevie Silver, We are pleased to
> inform you—

"But it said 'we regret'!"

"That wasn't you," said Thomas. "That was Starlotta!"

"*What?*"

"They went and put both letters in the same envelope."

"Oh!" I clapped a hand to my mouth. I'd got the scholarship and Starlotta hadn't. And I'd gone and read her letter! "Oh," I said, "that's awful!"

"No, it's not," said Thomas. "It's brilliant! You're going to be a STAR!"

"But what about Starlotta?"

"I thought you hated her?" said Thomas.

"Well…I don't exactly *hate* her."

"She was mean about the cat. She'd have let it die! Don't waste time feeling sorry for *her*," said Thomas. "Let's go and ring Mum and Dad!"

So I rang Mum and Dad ("We'll have a celebration tonight," promised Dad) and then I rang Steffi, and then Rosa and Dell. Steffi cried, "Oh, Stevie, what bliss!" Rosa said, "Hooray! I knew you'd beat the socks off her!" Dell said, "Great! So we're still the Gang of Four!"

They were all really pleased for me. But I kept thinking about Starlotta. I mean, I was sitting on her letter! She didn't know that she hadn't been offered a scholarship. When Mum came in at lunch time I asked her what she thought I should do.

"Shall I ring her?"

"Oh, I don't think so," said Mum. "I don't think she'd be very happy to know that you'd read her letter. Let me call the Drama Foundation, then they can put another one in the post and she needn't ever know."

So that was what we did.

When I went back to Starlight after half term, my head was way up above the clouds! I was Stevie Silver and I was going to be a S*T*A*R*.

All the same, I was a bit worried about what I was going to say to Starlotta. I know she is a total and utter pain, but in spite of what Thomas had said I couldn't help feeling just a *bit* sorry for her.

Well! I needn't have bothered. The minute she saw me, she came shrieking across the yard.

"Stevie, I'm *sooo* happy for you! I said to my uncle, now Stevie can have the scholarship. It was just *sooo* generous of him!"

I blinked. What on earth was she talking about?

"My uncle is going to pay for me!" gurgled Starlotta. "He just wanted me to try for the scholarship because he thought it would do me good."

Oh, ho ho! What she meant was, he'd been hoping she'd get one so that he wouldn't have to fork out.

I *could* have burst her bubble. I could have told her about the letter. But my head was too high up amongst the clouds! And anyway, it would have seemed a bit mean.

I'd been offered a scholarship! That was all that mattered.

Oh, yes! And I nearly forgot…we kept the kitten! We called him Star, short for Star Struck.

It's what my dad says I am!

Turn the page for
more books by
Jean Ure that
you might enjoy...

JEAN URE

Girls Stick Together!

£4.99   1 84121 839 1

The girlfriends are all going to different schools now. The gang meets every Saturday, but suddenly Polly finds she has other invitations, like to her new friend, Chloë's, party.

Who will Polly choose?
Will the girlfriends stick together?

£4.99   1 84121 843 X

Frizz is behaving very strangely.

Polly is worried that Frizz hates her new school and feels lonely without the rest of the Gang of Four.

But is Frizz feeling left out, or is she the grooviest girl of all?

More Orchard Red Apples

The Truth Cookie	Fiona Dunbar	1 84362 549 0	£5.99
Cupid Cakes	Fiona Dunbar	1 84362 688 8	£5.99
Chocolate Wishes	Fiona Dunbar	1 84362 689 6	£5.99
Utterly Me, Clarice Bean	Lauren Child	1 84362 304 8	£4.99
Clarice Bean Spells Trouble	Lauren Child	1 84121 920 7	£4.99
The Fire Within	Chris d'Lacey	1 84121 533 3	£5.99
IceFire	Chris d'Lacey	1 84362 373 0	£5.99
My Scary Fairy Godmother	Rose Impey	1 84362 683 7	£4.99
The Shooting Star	Rose Impey	1 84362 560 1	£4.99
Hothouse Flower	Rose Impey	1 84616 215 7	£4.99
Do Not Read This Book	Pat Moon	1 84121 435 3	£4.99
Do Not Read Any Further	Pat Moon	1 84121 456 6	£4.99
Do Not Read Or Else	Pat Moon	1 84616 082 0	£4.99
Stevie Silver – Stage Struck	Jean Ure	1 84121 782 4	£4.99
Boys Are OK	Jean Ure	1 84121 847 2	£4.99
Pink Knickers Aren't Cool	Jean Ure	1 84121 835 9	£4.99

Orchard Red Apples are available from all good bookshops,
or can be ordered direct from the publisher:
Orchard Books, PO BOX 29, Douglas IM99 1BQ
Credit card orders please telephone 01624 836000
or fax 01624 837033
or visit our Internet site: www.wattspub.co.uk
or e-mail: bookshop@enterprise.net for details.

To order please quote title, author and ISBN
and your full name and address.
Cheques and postal orders should be made payable to 'Bookpost plc.'
Postage and packing is FREE within the UK
(overseas customers should add £1.00 per book).

Prices and availability are subject to change.